Moonshine Ridge Mountain Men Volume 1

The McAlllisters

Rocklyn Ryder

Magpie Press

Copyright © 2023 Rocklyn Ryder

All rights reserved worldwide

No part of this book may be reproduced, uploaded to the Internet, or copied without permission from the author. The author respectfully asks that you please support artistic expression and help promote anti-piracy efforts by purchasing a copy of this book at the authorized online outlets.

This is a work of fiction intended for mature audiences only. Names, characters, places, and incidents either are the product of the author's imagination or are used fictitiously. Any resemblance to events, locales, business establishments, or actual persons, living or dead, events, or locales is purely coincidental.

Trusting the Mountain Man

The McAllister Men of Moonshine Ridge

About

Ash McAllister

My brothers and I grew up right here in Moonshine Ridge, running as wild as the mountains we live in. As an experienced part of the local volunteer rescue and recovery crew, I've recovered more than one vehicle that wasn't equipped for the four by four trails that wind through the rugged landscape. But when I pull a terrified young woman from a river crossing gone wrong, I know I'll never be able to let the curvy beauty go.

Hyacinth is new to more than the outdoors and when she trusts me to teach her about more than camping, I make sure she knows she's mine forever.

Call it insta-love, but the men of Moonshine Ridge fall fast, hard, and forever.

Rocklyn Ryder

They don't cheat, and they don't wait when they know they've found the right one.
Filthy-sweet happily ever afters in bite-sized stories, some swearing, lots of steam, and always a happy ending.

Ash and Hyacinth

Trusting the Mountain Man
The McAllister Men of Moonshine Ridge book 1
Moonshine Ridge
by
Rocklyn Ryder

Chapter One

Hyacinth

The drive in was bumpy. It took a lot of patience to maneuver over all the rocks but that's why I got a Jeep. Although, I admit, I thought it was going to be easier to get here.

When I saw the squiggly line on the map, I knew it wasn't going to be a paved road, but I did think it was going to be a road!

Now that I'm here with me and my car in one piece, it's perfect.

I stop pulling my gear out of the Jeep's back seat and take a moment to look around. The bumpy, dirty road to get here was so narrow and rocky, most of it on the side of a cliff with a very steep drop off, I didn't have time to appreciate the beauty of my surroundings till now.

Inhaling deeply I breathe in the fresh, clean, mountain air and survey the steep granite mountains surrounding me. The sky is a shade of blue I can't remember ever seeing before. Trees taller than any power poles back home fill in the narrow valley that's been carved over thousands of years by the river rushing down from the higher elevations.

And I am going to spend the next few days camped on the edge of that river.

Right here.

All by myself.

With no cell phone signal.

I look down at the phone in my hand--pictures after all--just to check. Nope. No signal. For the rest of the week it's just me, a tent, a sleeping bag, a camp stove, and lot of dehydrated food that I picked up in the camping section when I bought my tent and sleeping bag.

Speaking of which, I should get that tent set up before it gets dark.

Fortunately, it's a basic dome tent with only two poles that criss-cross at the top. Super easy to set up. Even though it did take me three times before I realized the poles had to thread through the fabric loops along the tent's seams.

Now the tent is standing and seems pretty sturdy.

Although I'm not sure what to do with this extra piece of material it came with. A rain fly? And there's another short pole that's supposed to go with that but I couldn't figure out how to put it on the tent, even with the instructions.

That's OK, I think I'm going to enjoy being able to see the stars through the screen panels at the top of the tent anyway.

Tossing the rain fly and the bag the tent came in back into the Jeep, I get to work on turning my little seven by seven foot vinyl igloo into a cozy home.

I unroll the sleeping bag and spread it out inside the tent on one side, add the cute little blow up camp pillow to the head of my bed and bring in the little gym bag I packed my clothes and toiletries in and set it beside the bed.

So far so good.

For my first time ever camping, I think I'm doing great.

Camping was something I always wanted to do but my parents weren't into the outdoors. In elementary school, my friend Stacy went with her whole family ever year for a whole week. I was so jealous, she always talked like it was the best time of her life.

Well, here I am finally.

Eighteen, a high school graduate, and ready to start checking off my bucket list. Starting with going camping, right here in Moonshine Ridge.

Well. Not exactly *in* Moonshine Ridge, but that's the nearest town to where I am now even though I left the idyllic mountain community in the rear view mirror about thirty miles back. It was a really cute town though. With hanging baskets of flowers on the sturdy pillars supporting the porch awning that covers the boardwalk in front of the historical nineteenth century shops on one side of the street and more flower baskets hanging from the ornate lamp posts on the other side of the street where modern a concrete sidewalk ran in front of newer, free standing shops built of masonry with big glass windows showing what was inside each store.

It's the kind of place I can see myself settling down in someday.

With camp set up, I decide to take advantage of the solitude and do something daring.

The late July sun is still hanging above the mountain peaks that circle the gorge on the West side and it's plenty warm enough out to make the river that runs just a few feet from my camp look mighty inviting.

Stripping down to my bra and panties, I make my way to the edge of the water where there's a small stretch of sandy beach that gently slopes below the river's edge.

I'm about to run right into the water when I get an idea. Nervously looking around--as if I'm not the only person for at least twenty miles out here-- I unhook my bra and let it drop off my shoulders before tossing it back on a nearby boulder. Then one more look around and I add my panties to the boulder too.

Then I run straight into the refreshingly cold water with a shout, a lot of giggling, and maybe just a little cursing when I pop back up from my quick dip under the surface.

This water is *cold*.

Ash

A cobalt blue Jeep Wrangler showed up on the other side of the river about two hours ago. Looks like one of the brand new models--bone stock.

No lift, no oversize tires, no rock sliders.

Whoever brought that thing this far up the Devil's Driveway is either a seriously skilled driver, crazy, stupid, or all of the above.

The downside to running the only sporting goods and hardware store in town is that it makes it damn hard for a man to actually get outdoors.

I've got five full days off while my brother, Birch, watches the store for me and I intend to spend them right here pretending to fish while I enjoy the sound of absolutely no other human being.

As soon as the thought has crossed my mind, the

peace is completely wrecked. The birds take flight around me as the canyon is filled with the sound of splashing and girlish giggles followed by an abrupt shriek.

Great. Just what I don't need--horny teenagers for camp mates.

No other voices follow the one feminine one though and I can't help my curiosity.

Standing up so I can see over the boulders strewn along the river bank, I search the opposite shoreline for the place where the Jeep was parked.

It's there all right, bright blue clashing with the forest's natural hues. Near the Jeep is now a bright yellow tent, a cheap one from a big box store that probably won't survive the night if the wind kicks up.

The tent's mesh roof vent is exposed to the sky too. I hope whoever put it up knows we'll probably get some rain at this elevation before mid-morning tomorrow.

My eyes continue to scan the shoreline, seeking the source of the splashing and shrieking, ready to get moving in a hurry if it turns out someone's in trouble.

A little further down the way from the highly visible camp, I spot what looks like clothing tossed onto one of the big boulders and sure enough, someone's swimming out in the big hole--the deep swimming hole where the river widens and the current slows down.

From where I'm standing, I can't make out the details of the woman in the water. Just the glint of deep red in her wet hair where the low afternoon suns hits it and the way it slicks down the back of her head and neck and then fans out around her, floating on the water's surface around her shoulders.

Then she swims back to shore and when her feet find the ground, she walks out of the water, ascending from the gradual incline of the beach like a goddess rising from the river.

My dick is immediately hard and my mouth is dry.

She's naked and dripping wet as she emerges from the river looking like something from my filthiest fantasies.

Nothing but smooth skin and luscious curves. Generous tits swaying with her steps and an ass that reminds my hands how empty they are.

Fuck me, man.

She uses both hands to wring water from her long, auburn hair, and then I swear I'm gonna jizz in my jeans right here when she turns around so she's facing directly toward me, tilts her head back and raises her arms, letting the warm sun light dry her body.

I never thought I'd be jealous of the fucking sun, but here I am staring like a fucking perv while I'm imagining drying her soft body with my tongue.

She obviously doesn't see me here. Her movements are totally innocent and unassuming, just a natural goddess taking advantage of the beauty of nature and feeling comfortable with what God gave her.

After a minute of letting the sun dry her skin, she grabs her clothes off the rocks and walks back to her camp without bothering to get dressed.

I watch that ass bounce and sway until she ducks into the ugly yellow tent and I have a chance to snap out of my daze.

Chapter Two

Hyacinth

Once I got over the initial shock of how cold the water was, it felt amazing. And the spot where I'm camped is right by a natural swimming hole where the water is so deep I couldn't touch the bottom even when I tried to dive down to it.

This was so worth all the planning, the long drive from the city, all the money I spent to buy camping gear--maybe I'll invest in some of that really expensive, high end stuff. When I decided that camping was how I was going to celebrate turning eighteen and finally getting to start exploring my love of the outdoors, I just wasn't sure I could justify spending four hundred dollars on a tent that looks exactly like the one at the big box store that only costs forty dollars--except the expensive one were all boring browns and greens and the cheap one came in this awesome sunshine yellow. And the sleeping bag says it's rated for thirty degrees which is plenty warm enough for nights in July.

Really. I can't believe that a sleeping bag that costs hundreds of dollars for the same temperature rating is going to be any better. It's not like I need it to squish down to the size of a softball.

Even if I was going backpacking--which maybe I'll do next, since this trip is going so well--I don't need my equipment to be the lightest and smallest available. I'm a pretty big girl, I'm not going to collapse if my pack weighs a few extra pounds.

I don't even bother putting my clothes back on after I let the sun dry me off some. I just wad it all into a ball and carry it back to my tent.

Who knew that being naked in the outdoors would feel so free? I love that I can just walk around out here and not feel self conscious about my body. There's absolutely no one to see me. I feel completely at ease out here and it is *liberating*.

Also, I'm starving.

After towel drying my hair and slipping on some warm, fleece pajamas, I head back out of the tent and work on screwing the little single burner camp stove onto the fuel canister. That part is easy enough but when I turn the valve and hold the match to it, it flares suddenly with a whoosh that scares me enough that I almost knock the stove over.

Great, Hy, you almost started a forest fire on your first night. I'm pretty sure that would be a bad sign for my future as an outdoorsy bad ass.

What I did knock over was the package of freeze-dried cheeseburger mac that I'd already opened in anticipation of adding boiling water to it.

These packaged camping meals weren't cheap either. Next time I'll just pack instant ramen.

I put the pot of water on the stove and let it heat while I sift through the box with my kitchen stuff in it for another dinner choice.

Chicken tetrazzini. I don't even know what tetrazzini is, but it's either that or lasagna and frankly, freeze dried lasagna in a bag sounds weird. I only got it because they only had the three types at the store and I figured I'd try one of each.

Twenty minutes later and I'm wishing I had gone with the lasagna.

The sun set fast, almost an hour before I expected it too, but I guess I didn't count on the fact that there's an entire mountain range between me and the horizon now. Once the sun dropped behind those craggy peaks, it took the temperature with it.

Now I'm staring at the dark circle where the fire ring is and kicking myself for not thinking to bring any wood for a fire.

In the daylight I'll scout around camp and see if I can gather enough for a small fire tomorrow night.

Speaking of fire. I raise my head and sniff the cold night air. There's a distinctive scent of campfire wafting through the mild breeze.

It doesn't take much effort to find the source. Just up river from me, on the other side, there's a faint but certain flickering light among the trees over there.

Looks like I have neighbors after all, I think. Hopefully no one that noticed me skinny dipping earlier.

The fire's warm glow is coming from a spot set back from the river bank up among the trees, out of sight from the river. I decide I probably got away with my experiments in public nudity and remind myself to keep my clothes on from now on.

It's still early but without a fire or any one here to talk to, there's no reason for me to stay up.

Tossing my mostly uneaten dinner in the bag I brought for trash--the upside of food that you eat out of foil pouches is that there are no dishes to do, I guess--I unzip the door of my tent and squirm my way into my sleeping bag.

I'm freezing cold and I can feel every stick and rock under the tent through the nylon sleeping bag, but when I look up through the mesh at the top of my tent I see the stars. More stars than I've ever seen in my life.

I swear I can see more stars right now than when I went to the planetarium on a field trip in the sixth grade.

It's so beautiful I stop noticing the lumps and bumps that make me feel like the princess and the pea, and after slipping my hoodie on over my pajamas I don't feel as cold.

The next thing I know I wake up to water dripping onto my face.

Ash

When the rain stops and the sun finally comes out, I get out of my tent and double check my camp.

Out here in the mountains, you have to be prepared for the weather to turn without notice and this morning's drizzle was barely enough to think twice about.

It did keep me in my tent though. With nothing on my agenda for the week, this isn't one of those backpacking trips where I have to pack up rain or shine at the crack of dawn to get to the next stopping point.

So I threw together some coffee under the shelter of my tent's vestibule and then lounged in my bag all morning, reading a book and enjoying the rain on the roof of the tent.

Now it's time to get out and stretch my legs. Maybe drop a hook in the water and see if I can catch me some dinner for tonight and, if I'm being honest, hope that it gets warm enough this afternoon that my neighbor decides to take another swim.

After checking my kitchen gear to make sure it stayed safe from rain, rodents, and bigger critters over night, I take the short walk past the tree line to the river's edge.

The river is running higher today. No doubt the higher elevations got more rain than we did, melted some of the remaining snow pack that's been clinging to the peaks late into the season this year. A few hours from now that snow melt is going to make its way down the canyon and the river's going to be uncrossable.

Peering across the water, I see the blue Jeep and the bright yellow tent.

While I stand here soaking up the sun, my copper-haired beauty steps out of her tent.

In the early afternoon light I can see her hair burning a fiery deep red and I can't help but imagine what it would look like spread out across my pillows at home, what the thatch of hair at the gates of her heaven will look like when she's wet and and needy while I suck her clit.

Now I'm standing on the edge of the river with a raging hard-on when my goddess spots me from the edge of her camp.

I raise my hand in a friendly wave but she only glares at me from across the river. Then she turns and hurries back to the tent that looks like it's about to collapse.

With the water rising over the course of the day, I know it won't be safe to head across the river and use any of the excuses I've come up with to meet the angel on the other side.

My truck's outfitted for the class four four by four trail that locals call the Devil's Driveway and I've got the experience to handle that river crossing when it gets high and fast like it will tonight, but that doesn't make it a good idea.

Judging from the way her tent is falling down and the amount of wet clothing she was wringing out, I'm starting to think she doesn't have much experience in the outdoors.

Eyeing her stock vehicle, I wonder how she even got it up the trail.

Granted, this is the last camping before the trail goes full class four; about two hundred yards farther up the trail from where she pulled over and she'd be stuck as hell. Maybe rolled. Definitely hiking her pretty ass all six miles back to the highway to flag someone down for help.

Then it'd have been up to me or one of the other Ridge Recovery crew to get up here and get her back to town.

That scenario plays out in my head and when I think of any of the other guys getting that call, I can't help the possessive growl that comes from deep in my chest at that idea; thinking how it could have been Glen or Rapid that had seen her first. They might be my buddies, but we might have had a parting of the ways if one of those assholes had gotten to my girl first.

Tomorrow, I decide, I'm going to go over there and introduce myself. Maybe give her some help with that tent, invite her to share a dinner of fresh cooked trout...ask her to marry me.

Somewhere in my soul I know my attraction to her isn't purely physical. She's mine and I need to claim her and make her my wife.

Knowing she's not in any danger of trying to leave before it's safe to do so--and that she's not going to get away before I have a chance to claim her--I head back to my camp, grab my fishing gear, and make my way up river to the other side of the diving rocks where the fishin's best.

Chapter Three

Hyacinth

After waking up with rain pouring through my tent's ceiling, soaking pretty much everything inside, I managed to get the rain fly thing at least covering the mesh panels so the water stopped coming in.

Not that it made a whole lot of difference since there was a huge puddle on the floor of my tent right where I'd left my clothes laid out for this morning. Part of my sleeping bag was wet too, but at least most of it stayed dry so I managed to wait out the rain without getting hypothermia.

Then, as if almost drowning in my own tent wasn't enough to have me thinking of packing it all up and leaving early, when the sun finally did come out I got a look at the guy who's camped across the river from me.

Now I'm pretty sure I'm alone out here with an ax murderer...or Bigfoot.

He was huge. Even from the distance between us, I could tell that he was easily over six feet tall, probably a lot over six feet, with wide shoulders and massively muscled arms that made his t-shirt look like it was painted on him. With thighs to match wrapped in faded denim.

His hair was dark and long, hanging down almost to his shoulders in dark waves blowing wild in the mountain breeze...and that beard.

I could barely even see his face, his beard was so bushy, but there was no mistaking the eyes that were staring straight at me while I was trying to wring out my wet things on the riverbank.

A shiver seizes my spine.

That guy is exactly the reason that women don't go out in the woods alone--a real mountain man that probably lives in a shack somewhere around here and only eats what he kills with his bare hands.

He was huge, he could probably strangle a moose if he needed to.

All day long my thoughts race like this, utterly obsessed with the mountain man across the river.

I imagine that he probably lives in a tiny little cabin that he built with his own hands. He probably has a bear skin rug on the floor that he killed with his own bare hands. He was probably sizing me up because he needs a wife that he'd--*gulp*--with his own bare hands.

I'm on high alert as I boil water and make the lasagna in the pouch and as the sun sets behind the jagged peaks to the West, I'm only mildly relieved when I see his fire dancing from behind the trees on the other shore.

At least I know he's staying on his side of the river--which, maybe I'm crazy, but it sure seems like it's running higher and faster than when I went swimming yesterday.

The lasagna isn't much better than the chicken stuff from last night and I'm starting to crave a real meal. A double thick cheeseburger with bacon and onion rings on the side.

Putting the pouch from the lasagna into the trash bag, I start thinking about the tavern in Moonshine Ridge.

It was a big building with rough-hewn log siding and windows all the way around so you could see the people enjoying their meals inside.

The sign outside it said "Only Mama Cooks it Better" with a hand painted hamburger, fries, and milkshake, so I know it was a family friendly restaurant and not just a bar even though it said "tavern" on it.

But it's dark now and that dirt road to get here was no joke. I don't want to try to navigate it after dark.

Besides, I am determined not to chicken out of my camping trip! It's only a couple more days of lousy food and being so cold at night that I have to wear all my clothes to bed, and unpredictable weather and scary looking mountain men that look at me like they are either thinking of cooking me and eating me or chaining me in a shack until I agree to become his wife.

Assuming a man like that waits till a woman agrees, that is.

Something moves in the woods outside my tent, putting my nerves on edge. Then a branch snaps and I swear it's either a grizzly or a lonely mountain man.

Either way it's all I need to convince me that it's time to get out of here.

Everything is shoved into the back of the Jeep in thirty seconds flat. The whole tent, the camp stove, the little ice chest with the milk for my morning cereal--all of it. Pretty sure I broke some tent poles while I was cramming the thing behind the front seats but I can get another tent. But first I have to live to go shopping again!

Throwing the Jeep into gear with the high beams on, I turn onto the hellish dirt road that brought me here and pray that I can get back to the highway in the dark, but when I reach the spot where the road is cemented where it crosses the river, things go sideways. Literally.

When I got here yesterday, it was fun to drive through the running water as it flowed over the dipped concrete but yesterday the water was only a foot high at best and flowing lazily across the road.

The river really is higher tonight. The water is up to my doors and the current smacks the passenger side with enough force that I feel the whole Jeep sliding sideways.

I hit the gas pedal but nothing happens. The engine revs higher but I'm not moving forward. Instead, I'm getting pushed farther sideways. I feel the tires drop off the side of that concrete under me onto the natural riverbed.

Now I'm tipped over at a crazy angle with the river pushing me like it's trying to roll the whole vehicle over. Water is starting to leak through the bottom of my door and everything is getting soaking wet.

I need to get out of the Jeep, but the door won't open against the water. I'm about to crawl over the door and out the window when headlights blind me through the windshield, aimed directly at me from the other side of the rushing water.

Ash

The unnatural glare of headlights splits through the darkness and I know it's her. Sure enough, she pulls out of the clearing where she's been parked like she's being chased.

Throwing the bucket of dish water from cleaning up after dinner on my fire, I grab my keys and head straight to the truck.

If she's really hellbent on getting out of here now, she's going to need to be winched across that river.

By the time I get in place though, it's already too late.

Her Jeep is too light and too low for the river right now and the current has managed to sweep it downstream so that the driver side tires are over the edge of the concrete wash. She's listing dangerously to the side and every time she revs the engine, I imagine she's coming closer to drowning the air in take.

Without thinking, I have the truck pulled up as close as I can safely get in the rushing water, pulling the winch line out and wading into the frigid current. The water is up to my waist and I have to put a lot of effort into keeping my feet under me so I don't get pulled down river and over the falls along with her Jeep.

This isn't safe but it is an emergency and I'm running on pure adrenaline now. The only thought in my head is to protect my girl.

Hooking the winch cable to the tow points under her front bumper requires submerging most of my upper body. Now pretty much all of me is soaking wet and even though I know it was the right thing to do, I'm regretting dousing that fire before I got in the truck.

Through the windshield I can see her face and damn but it hits me hard how terrified she looks right now, staring straight at me, her eyes wide as saucers and visibly gasping for breath through plump lips that were made for smiling and sucking cock--not for the panicked breaths she's gulping through them right now.

I pound on the hood of the Jeep.

"Stop!" I yell again.

Her eyes seem to register that I'm in front of her and if it's possible, they get even wider.

Bracing myself against her car, I push my way along the passenger side until I'm even with the windows--those damn canvas things that are fun as hell on a good day but not doing jack shit to keep the water from pouring over the edge of the half doors and filling up the cabin.

"Straighten your wheels back up," I yell through the zippered window.

Her head swings wildly toward me and then I swear she's about to shimmy out of the window on her side of the car. Holy fuck. If she does that, she won't stand a chance against the current and the next recovery happening on this mountain will be at the bottom of Diaz Drop.

My multi-tool is open and slicing through the vinyl window before she escape on her side. The cabin of the Jeep is filled with water now. I'm not sure this Jeep is going to survive tonight, but I'll be damned if she doesn't.

"Hey!" I shout at her as I slip into the passenger seat and grab hold of her arm, forcing her away from the driver side door and snapping her out of her panic. "Put it in neutral," I command when her eyes finally seem to focus on me.

She looks down at the shift lever like it's going to bite her and I reach over and grab the wheel with my left hand, spinning it so the tires are headed straight for my truck's headlights.

"Neutral," I say again, not having to yell quite as loud this time.

Her hand moves the lever and I reach up and hit the remote for the winch with my right hand while I steer from the passenger seat.

For a second I think it's a lost cause and my brain spins with a hail Mary plan B to grab her and bail out before the river sweeps the Jeep past hope, but then I feel the wheels find purchase on the rocky river bottom as the winch pulls us close enough to the shore to be out of danger.

That's when I realize the goddess in the driver's seat is crying so hard she can't catch her breath.

Hitting the remote again, the winch on the front of my truck stops turning.

"Brake," I tell her softly. "Can you put your foot on the brake for me, baby?"

Her foot moves to rest on the brake pedal but she's still sobbing uncontrollably.

I throw the gear shift into park and reach over to kill her engine.

"Hey," I turn and take her chin in my hand. "It's OK

now," I assure her as I turn her head toward me. "You're safe now, but we need to get you dried off and warm so you don't go hypothermic, OK?"

Her eyelids flutter a few times and I think she might faint on me, but then her eyes come into focus as she finally registers what I'm saying to her.

"Come on, baby," I say gently, "you can trust me."

Chapter Four

Hyacinth

"P-p-please don't hurt me."

I'm so cold my teeth won't stop chattering and I can't feel my feet.

If this guy is going to kill me there's not much I can do to prevent it.

He turns to look at me from the driver's side of the big pick-up truck he used to pull my Jeep out of the river. I can't read the expression on his face and that doesn't do a whole lot to inspire confidence when he tells me to trust him.

The look he shoots me from across the cab tells me he's offended.

"I'm not going to hurt you, baby," he tells me, "I'm trying to keep you safe and take care of you."

My jaw clacks uncontrollably from cold and fear and the only thing warm on my body are the new tears streaming down my face.

"D-d-do you need a w-wife?"

The look he gives me is not exactly a no and I'm pretty sure I'm never going to see my parents again.

Thoughts of the missing persons report flash in through my mind. I wonder if the authorities will find my Jeep and assume I was washed downstream. How long before I'm declared dead and they call off the search party?

Is my mountain man captor at least going to take good care of me while I'm chained in his shack or am I going only eat gruel for the rest of my life? What is gruel, anyway? I decide I don't want to know and new tears spill from my eyes.

"Here," he finally says as he parks the truck in a small clearing near a cozy looking camp. "I'm going to get the fire going again, but first we need to get you out of those wet clothes. Do you understand?"

He gets out of the truck and grabs something from behind the seat.

Great, I think, *here comes the rope*. My feet are still frozen numb. If I tried to run now I'd probably break my ankle, not to mention there's no way I could outrun this guy. Up close, he's not just huge, he's all muscle and looks like he can outrun a freight train.

I silently accept my fate as he makes his way to the passenger side of the truck where I'm still sitting, soaking wet on his leather upholstery and shivering so hard I feel dizzy.

The door opens beside me and he holds up a blanket which he wraps around me as he pulls me off the seat so that I'm standing right in front of him.

"I need you to strip down for me now, baby." His voice is so gentle when he talks to me. Deep and soothing. "Just go ahead and take off everything that's wet and then wrap yourself up in the blanket. I won't look."

He holds the blanket up like a curtain between us but I can't move. I'm shaking too violently and I've never felt so tired in my life. I feel my body starting to sink back against the truck.

"Whoa there."

The blanket wall comes down and he's catching me before I hit the ground as my knees buckle under me.

When I open my eyes again I'm wrapped up in a sleeping bag in front of a roaring fire. I can feel my feet and they don't feel like they're tied together.

I move my arms--also not tied up.

Seems like a good start until I realize I *am* butt naked in the sleeping bag.

"Good, you're awake," his deep voice says from near my head. "I'd really like it if you could drink some cocoa for me, baby."

Blinking rapidly, I sit up, clutching the edges of the sleeping bag around my shoulders and scooting like an inch worm till I'm turned around and looking up at him from a few feet away.

"Um, my clothes," I manage to spit out.

He looks at me and there's something about the caring look in his eyes that does something funny to my tummy.

"You were soaking wet and your body temperature was dropping fast from shock and the cold, I needed to get you dry and warm as quickly as possible." He speaks the words slowly and clearly like he's used to explaining emergency situations to people.

It makes me feel safe. *Er.* Safe-er. I'm still not convinced he's not a fugitive from justice hiding out in the mountains and there's still the possibility that he's going to hold me captive until I develop Stockholm Syndrome.

"I promise I did my best not to look."

Eh, not sure I believe that one based on the way one edge of his mouth quirks up when he says it.

"I'm a licensed E.M.T." he adds, much more seriously, "I work with the local rescue and recovery crew in Moonshine Ridge. You can trust me, I know what I'm doing."

Pulling the sleeping bag tighter around my shoulders I do relax but just a little.

"Thank you," I whisper, still not exactly sure what to make of this guy.

By the light of the fire, his face looks kind even behind that beard. His hair has been brushed out and pulled back in a pony tail that looks like it's still damp from the daring river rescue.

"I'm sorry," I add after thinking for a second.

His eyes widen and half a smile pulls up one side of his mouth. He has really nice lips, I find myself thinking, he should trim the 'stache so you can see them better.

"Sorry about what, baby?"

"For..." what am I sorry about again? Oh yeah, "For trying to get away earlier."

"My name's Ash," he smiles fully and extends his right hand over toward me.

I sneak my right hand out of the sleeping bag cocoon, doing my best not to show too much skin. "Hyacinth," I tell him shyly.

"Nice to meet you, Hyacinth," he tells me, his eyes dance with reflection from the firelight as he looks at me long and thoughtfully.

"I'm glad you didn't get away."

Ash

"Here, drink this and I'll find you something dry you can wear."

Handing her a mug of hot chocolate, I get up and

head back to my tent where I set out a pair of my sweat pants and a flannel shirt for her.

After she fainted back at the truck, my only thought was to get her out of her wet clothes and get the fire going so she could warm up.

I really didn't look--much. I was too concerned about how cold her skin felt to the touch and the bluish tint that was coming into her lips.

So I wrapped her up in my sleeping bag, laid her down next to me, and brought the fire back to life.

Hyacinth. I let her name roll in my mind.

She's still scared and I'm not sure if it's just the near death experience or me.

"Here," I say, handing her the clothes, "you can change inside the tent if you want."

"Thanks," she says, taking the clothes from me before I turn my back to her so she can get dressed privately.

Behind me, I hear the rustle of the sleeping bag as she stands and the soft sounds of her movements as she dresses right where she is by the fire.

"OK, you can turn around now." I hear her soft voice behind me say. She's sounding less shaky and when I turn back around, she's standing close to the fire.

My clothes are way too big for her. The sweat pants are rolled up at the ankles several times and the shoulder seams of the flannel shirt droop to her elbows, the hem dropping down to her knees.

Her dark red hair is hanging over one should, damp

and tangled and she's busy rolling up the sleeves of my shirt.

"Now that you're safe and dry," I say, bending over and picking up the empty mug from her cocoa and refilling it for her, "mind telling me what was so important that you broke camp and headed out this late at night?"

Hyacinth sits back down, arranging the sleeping bag under her and holding her feet out toward the fire.

Fuck. I didn't bring socks for her. She's barefoot. I bet her feet are ice cold.

Mixing another packet of cocoa into the next helping of hot water, I hand the mug back to her and drag my camp chair closer to her.

"Gimme your feet," I demand, making it clear it's not a request.

Her eyes go wide and I remember the way she looked when I ripped through her window earlier.

"Were you trying to get away from me back there?" I jerk my head toward the trail. "Is that why you were determined to launch yourself into the river and over the falls?"

Hyacinth looks at me over the rim of the mug and nods just barely.

"You really thought I was gonna hurt you?"

Her eyes dart toward the fire and she shrugs.

"I thought you were a mountain man," she tells me shyly.

That makes me laugh. I throw my head back and let the laughter roll it's way out of my throat.

"Well I'm definitely a mountain man, baby," I assure her when I get a hold of myself again, "but the last thing I'm ever going to do is hurt you."

It's a damn relief when her shoulders relax and she starts to giggle.

Finally, I feel like she might be starting to trust me.

Chapter Five

Hyacinth

When Ash leans back and laughs, I can't help but relax and laugh too. He might admit to being a mountain man, but he seems like a pretty regular guy now that I'm getting an idea of who he is.

He gave me warm, dry clothes to wear, and the hot cocoa has me feeling warmer and less shaky, not to mention the campfire. Now he has my feet in his lap while I lay back on his sleeping bag and enjoy the warmth and crackle of the fire while he rubs my feet with his huge hands till my feet are warm and I'm feeling tired.

"Your Jeep looked like it was pretty new," Ash says as

he switches to rubbing my other foot, "Doesn't look like it's had any mods on it. How'd you get back here?"

He's been explaining that the forest service road I took to get to the river is actually the beginning of a renown four wheel drive trail. Off roading enthusiasts come from all over to try to make it from Moonshine Ridge all the way to Paradise Point on the East side of the mountains from here.

"Very slowly," I tell him, and we both laugh together again. "The post at the turn off had a little picture of a Jeep on it, I have a Jeep. I thought it meant I was fine."

"You did really well considering its a stock Jeep and you don't have any experience," he tells me. "The road this far isn't as bad as it get from here on out, but I've pulled more than one off-the-lot SUV out of here when someone didn't understand that the sign that says "properly equipped vehicles only beyond this point' means lifted with thirty-five inch tires."

"Do you think it's going to be OK? My Jeep, I mean. It was my graduation present, I haven't had it very long."

"Yeah? You just graduated college?"

"High school."

His hands go still on my feet and he just stares at me.

We'd been getting along pretty well and I've been feeling really comfortable with him.

Now I sit up and tuck my feet under me with the sleeping bag gathered up over my knees.

"Fuck, baby, how old are you?"

"Eighteen," I say defensively. "And a half."

Something about Ash makes me want him to see me as an adult. As a woman. Not some little girl that he had to rescue from the river in the middle of the night because she doesn't know anything about the outdoors.

Something about Ash has me feeling all kinds of things that I'm not familiar with.

Slowly, he blows out a long exhale and fidgets his hands in his lap like he's expecting my feet to still be there. He stares into the fire for a a long minute.

"Well, the engine was still running when we got you to the shore, so that's a good sign. We'll check it out tomorrow and see if it's going to need anything more than a good cleaning out from the water damage to the interior."

"So you think I'll be able to leave tomorrow?" I ask.

Something changed and suddenly I feel awkward. I have a desire to get as far away from Ash as I can--and not because I don't trust him. No. Now it feels like he's pulled away from me and that has me feeling colder than the river he pulled me out of a few hours ago.

"No way." His voice is gruff and full of authority. "You are not driving that thing back out of here with an experienced spotter and a second vehicle with recovery gear. When your car dries out, I'll go with you."

"I don't want you to have to leave early," I tell him, feeling guilty.

He's been telling me about his home in Moonshine Ridge, about the outfitter's shop he runs there and about his family history in these mountains. He's been looking forward to this fishing trip for weeks. I don't want to be the reason he has to cut it short.

His eyes narrow as he looks at me. "I don't want you going alone, got it? I'll go when you go."

The way he smiles at me does more to warm me up than the fire has.

Ash

She wants to stay here. With me. I'm filled with pride that my girl is trusting me to protect her now.

Hyacinth's eyes flutter, fighting to stay open. Now that the adrenaline from tonight's adventure has dissipated and she's feeling safe and warm, she must be exhausted.

Thing is, her own gear is soaking wet and in her Jeep back at the trail. Which just leaves us with the one tent for the both of us.

"Come on," I tell her, reaching for her hand and pulling her to her feet, "let's get you into bed and then we can decide the rest tomorrow. How's that sound?"

Hyacinth looks up at me and then swivels her head to look around my small camp site.

"You're going to sleep in my tent tonight," I tell her. "I've got an extra blanket in the truck and I'll bed down in there for the night so you can have the tent to yourself."

There's no way I could sleep next to her curvy little body all night and keep my hands to myself. Best thing to do is crash in the pickup for the night, I want Hyacinth to get a good night's sleep--when the time comes, I want to make sure she's making her decisions with a clear head.

"You're sure about this? I'm sure there's room for both of us in here," Hyacinth says as I make sure she's comfortable in the tent.

I know there's room for both of us, I just don't trust myself to be so close to her and not touch her.

"I'm fine, Hy," I promise her, "I've spent plenty of nights in the truck before, I'll be fine. I'll see you in the morning."

"OK." She lays down with her head on my pillow and I zip up the bag so she won't have any drafts getting to her. "Hey Ash?" she calls softly as I back out of the tent and start zipping the door.

"Yeah babe?"

Even in the dark I can see how beautiful she is, her hair looking dark as it spills over the small camp pillow under her head, her smile shy as she looks at me with the sleeping bag pulled up and tucked tightly under her chin.

"Thank you for saving me tonight."

"No problem," I assure her. "Get some sleep. I'll see you tomorrow."

After washing out the cocoa mug and securing the food to avoid attracting critters, I douse the fire and make sure it's out before crawling into the cab of my truck.

With the bench seat cleared off, it really isn't so bad to spend a night in here. If I didn't have the tool box taking up so much space in the bed, I'd be able to stretch out under the stars back there. But it never occurred to me that I'd be playing the chivalrous role of giving up my tent so a pretty girl could get a good night's sleep.

It's not the cramped truck cab that's keeping me awake though. I can't get Hyacinth's innocent eyes and plump lips out of my head. The way she was looking at me while we were sitting by the fire, like she was thinking about me the same way I'm thinking about her right now. Like I'm not the only one who'd rather have her snuggled up tight against me in my tent.

My dick is so hard I can't sleep. Can't get comfortable. Can't stop thinking about claiming my girl and making her mine.

Now that I've touched her, felt those curves in my hands, even under the circumstances, I can't stop thinking about what she'll feel like when she's warm and wet and begging me to claim her.

The image has me going out of my mind with the need for relief.

Reaching down under the cover of the heavy wool blanket, I push my hand beneath the waistband of my sweatpants and grip my throbbing cock. It only takes a couple of quick jerks of my wrist and the thought of Hyacinth's pouty mouth in place of my hand before I'm emptying my balls onto the leather interior of my pick up truck.

It's a far cry from where my seed belongs--deep in Hyacinth's womb where it'll take root and grow our babies--but at least I can finally get some damn sleep.

Reaching into the glove box to grab some tissues, I mop up the mess and fade off into dreams that have me hurting all over again when I wake up to the birds singing at the crack of dawn.

Chapter Six

Hyacinth

The sound of birds singing all around me wakes me up, then I smell the delicious scent of fresh coffee and bacon wafting in from outside. The distinctive sound of campfire crackling lures me out of the tent despite the chill of the early mountain morning.

"Morning beautiful," Ash says as I join him by the fire.

He's crouched down next to the fire ring, tending to a large skillet that's filled with sizzling bacon.

My stomach growls.

"Coffee?" He asks, replacing several crispy strips from the pan with fresh pieces from a package that sits on a small table next to him.

Before I can answer, he has the handle of the coffee pot wrapped with a pot holder and is pouring the steaming hot dark liquid into a mug for me.

"There's some creamer and sugar on the tailgate so you can doctor it up," he tells me, handing me the mug and nodding toward where his truck is parked a few feet away with the tailgate down and set up as a makeshift table.

"I'll get started on the pancakes as soon as this batch of bacon is done," he tells me.

It's so different camping with Ash. I slept so much better in his sleeping bag with the padded mat underneath me. I didn't get one of those because I thought they were just a luxury thing, but Ash explains that sleeping pads are essential gear that provide insulation to keep you warm, not just padding to keep you from feeling every rock and stick under you.

"Although they do help with that," he says, giving me a wink.

The more I look at him, the more I fall in love with his quick smiles and the way his eyes crinkle at the corners when he laughs.

He looks a lot less like the kind of mountain man who lurks in the woods kidnapping young women and more like the kind of mountain man I'd like to get kidnapped by.

The pancakes are delicious, the bacon is amazing and Ash is quickly teaching me that camping is something I definitely want to keep doing. Especially with Ash.

We hike out to the trail to check on my Jeep and the rest of my stuff. The Jeep isn't starting and my gear is trashed. Ash puts a note on my windshield and we hike back to his camp.

"We'll give it another day and see if the Jeep cranks over," he tells me. "If it still won't start, I'll get one of the recovery crew to come up and help me pull it to town. Till then, you can keep the tent, and I've got plenty of food for both of us."

I don't want him to sleep in his truck again. I want him to share the tent with me. I was awake late last night thinking about what it would feel like to have Ash's hard body pressed against me in the dark. Wondering what it would be like to have his manhood hard against me.

Ash is the first man I've ever met that made me feel this way. Like I understand what it means to be a woman.

But I saw the way he cringed last night when he found out how old I am. It's pretty obvious that he's older than me, but I don't care about age. That's not what determines if people are compatible or not.

I know it matters to some people though and it seems pretty clear that Ash doesn't see me as woman but as a little girl he had to rescue from the river because she was too dumb to know better than to cross it when it was so high.

"So why was the river so bad last night anyway?" I ask while we prepare to make dinner.

I'm learning so much from Ash about how to make a fire, clean the fish he caught earlier this morning, and keep the campsite clean and organized so we don't accidentally invite a bear to dinner and to make sure the area looks untouched by humans after we leave; and I find myself wanting Ash to teach me about more than just camping on this trip.

"Storm from yesterday hit the high elevations harder than it did down here," he explains in that gruff voice that sends shivers through me every time he speaks. "The rain melts the snow pack up there and sends all that extra water rushing down the river valley. Takes a few hours for the water to make it this far downstream, but storms like that can raise a river several feet. Add that to the hydro electric plant's cycling of the water from Serenity Reservoir back up to the plant at Turtle Lake and you get what we had last night.

"If you'd gotten out of the Jeep, you'd be at the bottom of Diaz Drop by now."

"What's Diaz Drop?"

He gives me a look so deep I swear he can see through me. Those dark eyes go soft with a kind of sadness in them that tells me that whatever Diaz Drop is, the thought that I could have ended up at the bottom of it upsets him a lot.

Then the expression on his face clears and he points down the river where it turns out of sight.

"Seventy-eight foot waterfall just past that bend," he tells me. "Not one of those free fall kind where the water just spills over the cliff like getting poured out of a pitcher, the cliff angles out at a steep slope. Lots of rocks. Nothing goes over and makes it to the bottom in tact."

gulp

"What the hell made you break camp and try to drive out of here after dark with the river running so high, anyway?"

He sounds mad but the look in his eyes when he glares at me is all worry. Maybe the rough bark of his voice should make me feel scared of him, but instead, I feel protected. Like this man cares about me and wants to keep me safe.

Those feelings I've been having flutter up again. Something pulls in my lower belly and my nipples feel tingly.

"Something moved outside my tent," I confess. "I thought someone was trying to get me and I got scared."

"Who else did you think was out here in the middle of nowhere that would be trying to do you harm?"

My breath is coming shallow and I can't look him in the eye now.

"I saw you across the river yesterday," my voice barely a whisper, "looking at me."

Ash

"You're scared of me?"

Her words go straight through my heart like a dagger. This woman is everything I ever dreamed of having and she's so fucking afraid of me that she almost killed herself to get away. No wonder she was trying to climb straight into the river when I cut through her window last night.

Her pretty red hair shimmers in the morning sun as she shakes her head quickly.

"Not any more," she tells me.

When her eyes pull back up to mine, the bright blue I noticed last night has darkened a shade. I can hear the way her voice has gone breathy and shy.

I take a step forward, getting into her space.

"What do I make you feel now?"

Her eyes go stormy and I watch her little pink tongue sneak between her lips to wet them.

I know what she's feeling and I love knowing it's not just me. This pull to each other that has me knowing we belong together and has my balls aching to fill her up.

"I-I don't really know," she stammers out. "I've never felt like this before."

"Is your pussy wet?"

Her throat works in a hard swallow at my coarse

words but she doesn't flinch. Her head bobs up and down in confirmation.

One step closer to her and there's no space left between us now.

"Mind if I see for myself?"

Hyacinth stands still, letting me crowd her. Like I'm some kind of wild beast she doesn't want to scare off.

She's got no idea how close to the truth that is. Right now I'm feeling half feral, ready to pull her to me and take her roughly up against the side of my truck.

My lips hover close to hers as I move my hand down, my fingers grazing her breasts lightly to feel her nipples hardened against the fabric of my own flannel shirt. But I don't kiss her. Not yet.

My fingers pull at the waistband of the sweats pants and her breathing goes completely still as my hand moves between the soft cotton and along her bare skin.

Fuck me. She's not wearing any panties under my loaned clothes. I should have been prepared for that, everything she had on last night was soaked through, but it catches me off guard and my dick surges with so much need I almost come in my pants right then and there.

My fingers drag through a tuft of damp curls and then her swollen pussy lips.

"Baby, you're soaking wet." I groan.

A noise like a squeak makes it past her lips as my fingers explore her folds and when I tentatively dip one finger into her wet little hole I feel the tension in her body winding up.

"Damn baby, you're tight too."

"I've never...before."

"Never what, baby?"

I've got a damn good feeling I know what she means. Her tunnel is hot and wet and I can feel her walls pulsing around my finger begging me to release the tension I feel building in her body, but she's so tight there's no way anyone's ever been here before me.

"I've never. I mean no one has ever...I'm still a virgin."

Her eyes close tightly, and she tenses her jaw. The way she says it sounds like she's apologizing, but I don't want her to feel ashamed of waiting. Not when she was waiting for me.

"No one else has been here before me?" I want to hear her say it. "Not even like this?"

I drive my finger deep, and her hands fly up to my shoulders to brace herself. A little cry tears from her throat and she shakes her head back and forth, her eyes still shut tightly.

"Look at me, Hy," I command.

Her eyes barely open just a slit.

"Open your eyes, Baby, look at me."

Those baby blues pop open along with her mouth. She licks her lips again and then pulls that plump lower lip between her teeth in a way that makes her look as innocent as I can feel she is.

"Do you want me to stop?"

"No," she says breathlessly.

I'm finger fucking her harder now, testing a second finger and loving the way she arches her back, making a mewling noise in the back of her throat as her fingers dig into my shoulders.

"You like that, baby?" I'm panting now too, wanting to taste her so bad, wanting to thrust my hardness into her and mark her as mine forever.

She's moving with me now, riding my hand as I coax her higher.

"Ash, please don't stop," she rasps out, "it feels so good."

She buries her face in my shoulder, her hands clutching my shirt to keep her balance.

"Tell me, Hyacinth, have you ever made yourself come, baby?" I gotta know. I gotta know right now if this is something she's ever felt before.

Her head shakes against my shoulder and I can feel her channel starting to flutter around my fingers.

"You've never gotten off before, baby? Is that what you're telling me?"

A nod.

I fall backward against the side of the truck for support, my dick's so hard I'm seeing stars. No way I'm going to miss seeing her first orgasm as it rages across her face. I need a good look at my girl when she comes for me.

My free hand pushes up under the loose flannel

shirt and I fill my palm with her breast, squeezing and loving the way the soft orb overflows my grip. Then I pinch her nipple and pull it between my thumb and forefinger.

Hyacinth's head comes off my shoulder with a bolt, a shocked gasp escaping that pretty mouth of hers.

Her pussy is flinching around my fingers and I can feel how close she is, but she's fighting it. Tensing up and trying not to lose control.

"Ash," her eyes are wide and unfocused, there's lust there but also uncertainty. "It feels funny, I feel like--"

"Shhh, just trust me and let go, baby."

Before she can bury her head in my shirt again, I reach up and grab her hair, pulling her head back so I watch.

With a rough jerk I pull her tighter against me, pushing knee between her legs and putting more pressure against her needy little clit with the heel of my hand, giving her the extra friction that her body is desperate for.

"Come for me Hyacinth," I demand gruffly as she reaches the point where she can't fight it anymore. "Let me see how pretty you can come for me."

Chapter Seven

Hyacinth

The feeling that's been building inside me threatens to tear me apart. I've never come even close to feeling anything like this before and it's scary at first, but if Ash stops what he's doing I know it'll feel even worse.

I try to fight it, it feels like I'm going to lose consciousness and I don't want this feeling to stop but then Ash has me pulled so tightly against his body and he's telling me it's OK to lose myself in it.

When he tells me to come for him, I explode against his hand. My whole body shudders and convulses and I can hear my own voice screaming Ash's name back at me as it echoes off the mountains around us.

It feels like I just fell apart and then suddenly found myself back together again, clinging to Ash as he runs his hand down the back of my head, smoothing my hair into place and letting his hand rest at the small of my back.

He doesn't let go of me as he withdraws his hand from between my legs. He holds on to me, keeping me close to him, his eyes are the deepest shade of brown I've ever seen as he looks at me with a mix of pride and hunger.

"Like honey," he says in a low growl as he raises his hand to his mouth and licks my essence of his fingers. "Fuck, baby girl, you've got me addicted already. I hope you know that."

He reaches down with both hands and grips my ass, pulling me up to him with my legs straddling him till my sensitive sex rests against the hard ridge of his manhood.

"Feel that? That's what you've been doing to me ever since I saw you across the river yesterday." Ash's voice is a growl against my ear. "You have no idea how much I need you, Hyacinth. Tell me you want me, baby. Tell me you want to be all mine."

Sliding my hand between us, I reach down and feel him through his jeans.

"That's because of me?" I ask in wonder. It's just so hard for me to believe that I could be reason this huge, strong mountain man looks like he's about to snap.

"All you, baby," he hisses through clenched teeth when I run my hand down his hard length. "That's all yours, whenever you want it."

I feel my pussy clench at what he's saying.

"I want it now, Ash," I whisper.

"You sure?"

His face is close to mine and I can make out the chiseled cheekbones and the square jaw under his beard. I'm fascinated by the way he's looking at me, like he's on fire and I'm a glass of water.

My hand presses into his hardness again and his eyes flutter, his fingers sinking into my hips as he pulls me closer so I can feel that steel rod pressing against the same place where he was touching me earlier, making me want to squirm till I'm straddling him.

But we're still leaning up against his truck. He's so much taller and bigger than I am, there's no way I can get myself where I need to be in order to relieve the ache that's beginning to grow inside me again.

I nod firmly and Ash's mouth covers mine.

His beard is soft against my skin but his lips are so warm and firm as they move against mine, commanding me to open for him and let him slip his tongue inside.

I get totally lost in my first real kiss.

Ash's tongue glides against mine, inviting me to match his movements. His lips caress mine, moving hungrily, his teeth occasionally catching my tongue or my lip between them with gentle bites that make my whole body crave his touch.

I want his hands on me. I want his mouth everywhere. I want to feel what it's like to have a man inside me--to have Ash inside me.

His hands wrap around the backs of my thighs and he lifts me easily, settling my throbbing pussy up against his hardness so that I feel it rubbing against my needy pussy with my legs wrapped around his waist tightly as he carries me to the tent.

"Lay down, baby," Ash instructs, spreading the sleeping bag out underneath me and unbuttoning the flannel shirt he lent me.

"Your tits are beautiful," he mumbles against my breasts as he pushes the flannel aside and goes straight for my breasts. His hands wrap around me and knead the generous flesh, his mouth locked down on first one nipple and then teasing the other the same way with quick flicks of his tongue and gentle bites until both are hard and sensitive when he drags his thumb across them.

He keeps making his way down my body, stopping to lay tender kisses across my tummy that have me losing my self-consciousness. Instead, Ash has me feeling beautiful and sexy and I want to be those things for him.

"Oh baby," he groans into my sex as he inhales against me while his hands drag the loose-fitting sweat pants over my hips and down my legs till I'm completely naked from the waist down.

"Spread your legs for me baby," he says in a voice that's gone husky and rough sounding, "I need to see this pretty pussy."

Ash

Hyacinth is perfect. She may be young, but her body is all woman, soft and ripe for taking my seed.

Lying back on the rumpled sleeping bag, my flannel shirt unbuttoned and opened and completely naked except for that, she's on full display for me. From her pale pink nipples poking out straight and hard, to the thatch of deep red curls pointing the way to heaven.

Leaning in, I inhaled deeply, learning my woman's scent and letting it intoxicate me before indulging in my first taste of her.

When she relaxes and lets her legs fall open for me, I can see her virgin pussy glistening with evidence of her need.

"Fuck, Hyacinth, your little pussy looks like it's begging for me to fuck it." I strip my shirt off over my head and lean over her, first to kiss her lips, and then lower to finally get a taste of her sweet little cunt. "Is that true, baby? Do you want me to fuck your sweet little pussy for you?"

Hyacinth moans and wiggles her hips but she doesn't answer me.

"You gotta tell me you want it, baby, tell me you want my hard cock filling you up."

"I want that, Ash, I want your cock."

"That's my good girl," I croon into her slick folds. "I'm going to give you what you want, but I want to taste your cum on my tongue first."

My tongue drags through those petals that are blushing a dark pink and swollen with desire, down to her tight hole and then back up to suck on her extended little bud while I manage to wedge my wide shoulders even further between her legs, forcing her thighs wider.

It doesn't take long till she's writhing under me, tilting her hips up to ride my face while I stretch her tight little tunnel around two of my fingers, stroking her sensitive spot from inside while I tongue her clit till Hyacinth arches her back and screams for me again.

It's a sound that goes straight to my dick, causing it to throb painfully.

"Baby, I want to give you a minute to recover, but I need to be inside you," I manage to gasp out as I kick off my boots and strip my jeans and boxer briefs.

Positioning myself between her thighs, now fully

relaxed and limp from her orgasm, I kiss her deep, letting her taste herself on my tongue.

"I'm not wearing anything, and I'm guessing you're not on the pill, so if we get pregnant we'll just have to accept that, but I need to feel you on my bare skin. Understand?"

Hyacinth's eyes widen and she inhales sharply at what I'm saying.

"Hyacinth, baby," I lay my forehead against hers, forcing my words between gritted teeth while I do my best to stay in control. "I knew you were mine the minute I saw you. If you don't feel the same way, you need to say so now because once I have you, I'm never letting go. Do you hear me?"

"I'm talking marriage, babies, building a life together. Tell me that's what you want too, Hy, tell me you want that with me and I'll give you whatever you want."

Maybe I'm not playing fair, but I reach between us and press my thumb against her clit, priming her for what's coming.

She moans, moving against my pressure and looks up at me with heavily hooded eyes.

"I do want that, Ash," she whispers hoarsely, "that's what I want too, with you, Ash, only with you."

It's a fucking good thing she's telling me that, or else I don't know what I'd do. I'm a man possessed, every nerve in my body is on fire as I line the throbbing head of my cock up with her entrance, sliding through her folds to coat myself in her slickness before easing my way inside.

Going slow uses up every ounce of self control I have left, but my girl's a virgin, and I know she needs me to be gentle with her till she gets used to taking my cock.

"Ash," she moans under me. Her hands slide down my back and grip my hips, pulling me deeper. "Don't tease me, I need you all the way inside me."

Fuck me. I don't need to be asked twice.

"I don't want to hurt you, baby."

"Do it, Ash, please. Get it over with and make me feel good."

I surge forward. Pushing through the resistance of her innocence all the way to the root of my dick and pause. Holding Hyacinth tightly, waiting till she's ready to move.

As soon as she does, I pull back, letting her feel all of me and loving that little cry of disappointment at feeling me leaving her before thrusting back into her heat again and again building us both up until I know she's ready.

"Come for me, Hyacinth, I need to feel you coming on my cock." Reaching between us, I thumb her clit and she unravels so beautifully for me I don't make it through her full release.

One spasm of her channel tightening around my cock has me going off like a rocket, emptying my balls deep in her womb and leaving me spent.

"I love you, Hyacinth. Stay in Moonshine Ridge with me," I whisper against her cheek as I hold her against me, "be my wife."

She makes a happy little sound in my arms and then turns to look back up at me.

"I love you too, Ash. Take me camping for our honeymoon."

Epilogue 1

Three Months Later

Hyacinth

My husband keeps a grip on the roll bar above his head as I position the Jeep so the tires take the last rock in the trail without doing damage to the body. The Jeep's front axle comes down with a jolt and I hear the crunch of the rock against the body protecting rock sliders.

"Oops," I tell Ash, laughing as I keep moving till we reach the edge of the water up at Serenity Reservoir.

"You did great, baby," he tells me, leaning across the front seat to give me a kiss. "You're a natural."

My Jeep dried out and we got it back home. It barely needed any work done after I tried to drown it in the river.

Now it's got a six inch lift with thirty-five inch off road tire, a winch on the new bumper, and the rock sliders that replaced the running boards.

This isn't our first trip back up the Devil's Driveway, but it's the first one that where I did the driving.

Of course, we have a chase vehicle coming up behind us, two of Ash's brothers, Birch and Cedar are also joining us for the weekend camping trip.

Ash and I tied the knot two weeks after we got back from that fateful camping trip. It took us that long to get me moved in with him in Moonshine Ridge. Then we set the date for the soonest that the people most important to us could be there for our big day.

A small ceremony at his brother, Cedar's, lodge and tavern--yup, that's right, it turns out that the cheeseburger I wanted so bad that night is made by Cedar himself--and for our honeymoon, Ash took me to Yosemite National Park where we stayed in the fancy resort for a couple of nights, and then took a backpacking trip into the Sierra Nevada mountains.

We didn't get pregnant that first camp out--or the next--but I wanted to bring the Jeep up here this weekend because I'm not sure when the next time we'll be able to take it out is going to be, between the changing seasons and the little bean growing in my belly now.

"Looks like you kissed the bumper, baby," Ash grins, pointing at a small dent under the corner of the rear bumper where I most likely got too close to the side of the mountain.

It's fun crawling over the rocks in the trail, but I hate the stretch where there's nothing but sheer drop on one side.

With a shrug, I grab his hand and tug him toward me till his arms go around me and he bends down to kiss me.

Later we'll sneak off on a night hike for some private time away from his brothers, but right now, I only have a little bit of time to share my news. I can already hear the purr of Birch's diesel engine just around the bend.

"I want to tell you something before your brothers get here." I look up into my husband's brown eyes.

"Is everything OK?"

"Everything is fine," I assure him, "I just wanted to thank you for all the modifications you did on my Jeep."

Another brush from his lips and he gives me a smile, "Of course, babe, I want to make sure it's got everything you need for getting around on the mountain."

"Well, it does need one more thing then," I tell him with as straight a face as I can keep.

Ash looks over at the Jeep, and back at me with a puzzled expression.

"What else are you going to need, Hy?"

"A baby seat," I tell him, trying so hard not to crack a smile.

It takes a minute and then understanding dawns.

He's got me off the ground and swinging in a circle and then his mouth is on mine.

"Get a room!" Cedar's voice booms over the forest landscape as he climbs out of the passenger side of Birch's truck.

"I didn't drive up that god-forsaken death road to watch you two make out all weekend," Birch grumps as he slams the driver side door.

"Fuck you!" Ash yells at his brothers. "You jealous bastards better get used to it, this woman is carrying the next generation of McAllister men."

Epilogue 2

Five Years Later

Ash

Family camping trips are getting hard to plan and even harder to handle now with all of us McAllister men married and a growing herd of grand kids for my folks to chase after.

"Maybe grandma would like to hold her for awhile?" I lean down and whisper in my wife's ear.

Hyacinth gives me a look that says she knows what I'm up to, but she's not arguing. She hands our littlest over to my mom's eager arms and baby Bluebell doesn't even fidget in her sleep.

"We're just going to go for a walk, Ma," I explain.

Mom waves a hand at me from under my sleeping daughter. "Take your time," she says.

Bluebell is the current baby in the growing McAllister brood at a little less than six months old and we barely have a chance to hold our own daughter when the grandparents are around. But from the looks of Jasmine as Cypress stuffs another pillow behind her back, it won't be long till Bluebell has some competition for Grandma's attention.

The whole clan is down at Turtle Lake. It's not the solitude of a back country campsite, but the campground here has plenty of room for all of us and the lake has life guards on duty that have me and Birch feeling more at ease with letting the boys run wild.

"You're bringing a pack for a quick walk?" Hyacinth teases, looking at the bulging day pack I'm carrying.

"Maybe I brought a blanket and some snacks," I answer.

"Is this quick walk going somewhere in particular?"

"Maybe I know a secret spot." I grin.

My girl giggles and snakes her arm around my waist. After five years together, my wife knows me all too well.

"Please tell me this secret spot is some place secluded enough to to get naked in," she tells me, her voice going husky in the way that lets me know she's on the same page I am.

"Secluded enough for me to fuck another baby into you," I whisper in her ear as we hike.

"I got fixed when I had Bluebell," she reminds me, slapping at my arm playfully.

A growl rumbles through me as I steer her toward

the lightly used hiking trail that leads to a spot along the stream bed about a half mile up that's just perfect for a private dip in the cool water after getting sweaty with my girl.

"You know that's not going to stop me from trying, baby," I tell her, giving that luscious ass of hers a quick pat as she hurries along the path in front of me.

After two boys, we finally got our girl with Bell and decided to hold at three, so Hy got her tubes tied when she had Bell.

And that's just fine by me, but watching my girl's ass swing side to side as she hikes up the trail just ahead me has my dick just as hard and ready as she ever has.

You can believe, I am never going to stop trying.

Next in the McAllister Men of Moonshine Ridge

Birch:

Gossip and lore run deep in places like Moonshine Ridge, where the families that live here go back as far as the town itself.

Magnolia came here asking questions that I'd rather not know the answers to. Her distant aunt-- a mail order bride that arrived in the 1800s with a contract to marry my own ancestor-- disappeared under mysterious circumstances, and my family name has had a shadow hanging over it ever since.

As soon as I lay eyes on the innocent young newcomer to town with her soft curves and big blue eyes, I know she's mine. So I can't turn her down when she wants me to help her discover the truth that links our family history.

The only family history I want to talk about is the one I plan on making with Maggie and the babies I'm aching to put in her belly.

If Magnolia finds out that seven generations of local gossip is true will she still want me, or will she leave Moonshine Ridge and forever associate the McAllister name with murder?

Discovering the Mountain Man

The McAllister Men of Moonshine Ridge

About

Birch McAllister

Gossip and lore run deep in places like Moonshine Ridge, where the families that live here go back as far as the town itself.

Magnolia came here asking questions that I'd rather not know the answers to. Her distant aunt-- a mail order bride that arrived in the 1800s with a contract to marry my own ancestor-- disappeared under mysterious circumstances, and my family name has had a shadow hanging over it ever since.

As soon as I lay eyes on the innocent young newcomer to town with her soft curves and big blue eyes, I know she's mine. So I can't turn her down when she wants me to help her discover the truth that links our family history.

The only family history I want to talk about is the one I plan on making with Maggie and the babies I'm aching to put in her belly.

Rocklyn Ryder

If Magnolia finds out that seven generations of local gossip is true will she still want me, or will she leave Moonshine Ridge and forever associate the McAllister name with murder?

Call it insta-love, but the men of Moonshine Ridge fall fast, hard, and forever.
They don't cheat, and they don't wait when they know they've found the right one.
Filthy-sweet happily ever afters in bite-sized stories, some swearing, lots of steam, and always a happy ending.

Birch and Magnolia

Discovering the Mountain Man
The McAllister Men of Moonshine Ridge book 2
Moonshine Ridge
by
Rocklyn Ryder

Chapter One

Magnolia

Stepping off the transit shuttle in front of the general store almost feels like going back in time.

Moonshine Ridge is a quaint mountain town set among tall pines with a backdrop of steep mountains looming above. It's easy to imagine the way it must have look in the 1800s, the day my distant aunt Eliza stepped off the stage coach to meet the man she was going to marry.

The town is cute. With maybe three blocks of commercial buildings lining the main highway which also serves as the town's Main street.

I pick up my hand and wave at the woman who's been watching me like a hawk from inside the general store since I stepped off the shuttle.

I guess I found the town busy-body.

The bus pulls away from the curb and circles the

block to make its way back down the highway to the bigger town at the base of the mountain, committing me to the week I have booked at the lodge here in town: Shuttle service only comes up to Moonshine Ridge on Tuesdays.

What's not so easy to imagine about that day in 1871, is what happened to the young mail order bride that traveled across half the country to get here. Because my great, great, great, great, great, aunt never married Brodie McAllister.

Her trail stops right here, in Moonshine Ridge right after the travel documents say she arrived safely and was collected by her husband to be-- and was never seen again.

It's the one big mystery in my genealogy research and for some reason, I feel compelled to find out what happened to her.

That's why I came all the way across the country too. To see this historic mountain town for myself and find any trace that's left of a relative that went missing here over a hundred years ago.

According to the sign hanging from the awning, the place next to the general store with the nosy old lady is the local sporting goods retailer. When I get close enough to read the small signs taped inside the glass door panel, I find out that this is where one goes for fishing licenses, hunting licenses, maps, and information for the local tow truck and recovery services.

Inside I see a pregnant woman sitting in a chair by the counter while a huge man with a beard fusses over her. Another man watches from a few feet away and my belly does a flip flop at the sight of him.

They sure know how to grow 'em here, I think to myself, looking at the mountain men inside and envying the redhead with the baby bump that doesn't look like it's got that much longer to go.

Across the street, I spot the local historical center among the row of storefronts running along the stretch of highway that double as Moonshine Ridge's main street and head that way. It seems like as good a place as any to start my search.

Birch

Walking out of local sporting goods store that my brother, Ash and his new wife, Hyacinth run here in town, I catch a glimpse of thick, dark curls bouncing above a luscious ass and a pair of thick thighs in a pair of those jeans so tight they look like they're painted on.

She's not from Moonshine Ridge, that's for sure. I've lived here my whole life. Hell! My great something grandfather was one of the men who founded this community back when it was just a mining camp in the late 1800s.

I know all the full time residents of Moonshine Ridge and if I'd ever seen this particular cutie before, you can damn well be sure that I wouldn't still be single.

The curvy beauty is headed into the historical center across the street and wouldn't that just figure.

I'd been hoping to spend my day off tipping a few pints over at the tavern bar, watching whatever game they've got on this afternoon, and ribbing my other brother, Cedar, who runs the lodge and tavern, about the pretty new waitress he's obviously had eyes for since she showed up on the mountain a few weeks back.

The sawmill has been in my family since it was built in the last 1800s, after most of the gold in the surrounding mountains had been hauled out of here. It's a small operation, but still sees steady business after all these years. Unfortunately, small means not a lot of man power to take over so the boss man can take time off.

After bringing on a new man awhile back, I finally have a chance to take a couple days off a week without having to shut the whole operation down to do it.

The last place I want to spend my day off is in Mable Hart's local history museum.

That old woman has had a grudge against the McAllisters going back to when she and my nan were in school together. I've never understood it, I just try to avoid it.

But since that's where the woman who's bound to be my destiny is going, looks like that's where I'm headed too.

Chapter Two

Magnolia

When I walk through the door, a bell chimes and I see a woman's gray head pop up from behind a computer screen at a desk behind a long counter.

"Can I help you?" she asks without getting up.

"Um, I hope so," I answer, heading toward the high counter at the back of the room. "I'm looking for information about a relative."

"Living or dead, dear?"

"Most definitely dead by now," I answer with a light laugh, "she came to Moonshine Ridge in 1871."

"Uh huh." The woman still hasn't bothered to get up and meet me at the counter, choosing instead to peer around the edge of her computer monitor, looking at me through a set of red-framed glasses that clash with the bubble gum pink lipstick that doesn't suit the octogenarian's coloring.

In the back of my brain I tick off "eccentric old lady" on my internal small town bingo card to go with the busy body in the general store.

"Well, the town wasn't officially founded till 1878, you know. We don't have census records before then. Do you have any other information on her? Husband? Children? Date of death?"

"No," I answer, "none of that. Just the date she arrived by coach."

Obviously my local historian has decided I'm wasting her time. She fixes me with a glare that says as much and I start to think that I came all the way to Moonshine Ridge for nothing.

Maybe my distant aunt's trail really did stop here without leaving even a hint of what happened to her.

"Do you at least have a name?" The woman's voice teeters on the edge of politeness and impatience.

"Eliza," I answer, "Eliza Manchester."

I guess I finally said something interesting.

The woman, who's name plate on the edge of her desk reads "Mable," takes her hands off her keyboard and rolls her chair back from her desk. As she stands-- all five foot tall of her-- she reaches up and slides the red glasses down her nose and then off completely as she stares at me.

"And who would Eliza Manchester be to you?"

"My aunt," I say, "great, great great, great, great, aunt." I count the greats off on my fingers to make sure I get them all.

Mable finally joins me at the counter, fixing me with a gaze that's surprisingly cool for her deep brown eyes.

"She was supposed to marry a Brodie McAllister," I begin but Mable cuts me off.

"It was still technically called Hartsgold Gulch at that time," Mable is sure to let me know.

"Oh, I didn't know the town ever had a different name" I tell her, genuinely interested.

Mable guffaws and shakes her head, "Neither did the carriers for the postal service," she shares, "no one knew where to take the mail that was addressed to Hartsgold and pretty soon the post office officials changed the name to Moonshine Ridge."

"Interesting," I say, "but how does that help with finding out what happened to my aunt Eliza?"

"It doesn't," Mable scoffs, "I was just saying that the town wasn't meant to be named for the still."

Still? This is news to me. When I'd first found the name Moonshine Ridge, I'd assumed it was named literally-- after actual moon shining on the high mountain peaks surrounding the settlement.

But then again, I was never researching the town. My interest is only on filling out the parts of my family tree that were never going to come from stories passed down over generations.

"Ooookay," I draw out, not knowing the appropriate response and hoping Mable has relevant information to help with my search. "So do you have any information about what happened to Eliza Manchester after she arrived in Moonshine Ridge-- or Hartsgold Gulch-- whatever it was back then? Because I know she didn't marry Brodie McAllister."

"She definitely did not," Mable mutters with a hint of contempt that has me thinking there's a story there, but before I can ask what it is, the bell on the front door chimes.

Mable's eyes narrow and a Cheshire cat grin sneaks across her garishly pink lipsticked mouth.

Curiosity gets the better of me and I turn around to see who it is she's looking at with such keen interest and not very well concealed contempt.

The man standing in the doorway is so big he blocks out the view of the street from the glass-paned door behind him.

My mouth goes dry when I get a good look at the man I only briefly saw earlier when I was creeping on him through the sporting goods store window.

He's even taller than I'd guestimated, and his checkered flannel shirt is tucked in neatly to the waistband of a pair of faded blue jeans that are loose at the waist and tight across his tree-trunk thick thighs and ending at a pair of brown leather work boots that look like they've been worked hard.

"Birch, this is..." Mable pauses, waiting for me to fill in the blank with the name she never asked for.

"Magnolia," I say. It comes out all breathy like I just ran a marathon and I feel my cheeks warm and redden under his glare.

His eyes have been pinned on me and only me since I turned around. It's like Mable doesn't exist.

"Magnolia, and she's here to find out whatever happened to her great great great aunt--"

I don't fault her for skipping some greats, but I notice the way Birch's eyes flicker toward the old woman and a jaw muscle flinches under his beard as she pauses, no doubt for dramatic effect, before finishing the sentence.

"-- Eliza Manchester. Since you and your brothers are directly descended from Brodie, maybe you can help her out?"

Birch

The old biddy knows I don't want to talk to anybody about Eliza damn Manchester or any of the theories about what happened to her back in the 1800s that led to her disappearing instead of marrying my great great great grandfather Brodie McAllister.

It's been a source of gossip here on the mountain for generations and I've never been comfortable with shadow it's cast over my family's good name and our history here in Moonshine Ridge.

And Mable knows it.

The thing that's keeping me from telling the old bat to shove it is the same thing that brought me into the historical society's local museum to begin with. The angel looking at me from across the room now with hope written in her big blue eyes.

She's cute as damn button, with a thick fringe of bangs cut bluntly over her brows and a set a lush rosy lips that make my dick twitch in my jeans like a damn teenager, and the way she's looking back at me makes it easy to ignore the smirk on old lady Hart's smug face.

As soon as those baby blues meet my gaze, the only word ringing inside my head is *mine*.

My blood's boiling hot, but for once it's not Mable's orneriness chaffing my hide. No, right now my temperature is running high because all I can think about is the natural perfume wafting off the sweet flower in this dingy little space that passes for a museum of local history.

I don't know why this curvy goddess is here asking about ancient history that I'd just as soon let die on the grapevine it's been traveling for over a century now, but if it means getting to spend time with her, I'll draw out my entire family tree for her...because she and I are going to be the next branch.

It's clear that Mable Hart is dying to fill my girl's head up with generations of gossip about my ancestor and the cloud that's hung over my family name ever since his mail order bride vanished without a trace as soon as she arrived here in Moonshine Ridge in the 1870s.

Mable smirks at me. "I do know a few people who would be happy to talk to you about Eliza and fill in the blanks on what most likely happened after she arrived on the Ridge. Let me just give Vera a call and see if she's available."

My angel's eyes never leave mine as Mable prattles on about calling in Vera Jones.

The last thing I need is for those two gossips to fill my girl's head with their version of what happened to Eliza Manchester.

I don't want Magnolia to think poorly of my family name. I want her to wear it with pride when I make her mine.

If this sweet southern blossom needs to hear what likely happened to her distant aunt so long ago, I want her to hear it from me.

"I'll be happy to tell you what I know about your aunt Eliza," I tell Magnolia and enjoying the shocked look on old lady Hart's face.

Holding out my hand toward the beauty, I beckon her to come with me.

"Let's head over to the tavern," I tell her, pleased when she moves toward me and takes my outstretched hand. I have to hold my breath for a second when her fingers touch mine. The electric shock from our first contact shoots through me and my dick jumps in anticipation.

"Best burgers this side of the Rockies," I tell her with a grin, "and chili cheese fries to die for, my treat. Name's Birch by the way," I add as I hold the door open for her.

"I caught that, thanks," she says, smiling up at me and lighting my whole world up, "you can call me Maggie."

"Maggie," I repeat, practicing the feel of it on my tongue. Noticing the small overnight bag she's carrying, I reach down and take it from her. "Let me get that," I say when she looks up at me questioningly.

Then she smiles again and it makes me puff my chest out with pride at winning another one of her sweet smiles.

I let the door to the historical center slam shut with a clang of the little bell and Mable Hart's dropped jaw behind it.

"I get the feeling Mable doesn't like you?" Maggie asks as I lead her across the street to the tavern.

Her voice is sweet and melodic and there's a tinge of sarcastic humor to her statement that makes me think she picked up on the situation pretty quick.

Chuckling under my breath I give her hand a light squeeze and explain without getting too far into it.

"Mable likes drama," I say, "and she knows the gossip about my family history gets under my skin in a way that my brothers don't seem to share. You showing up askin' about Eliza Manchester just as I was coming in to meet you was perfect timing for her to stir the pot."

"You were coming to meet me?"

She looks so sweet and innocent, staring up at me with those big blue eyes like she can't believe that a man would cross the street just to talk to her.

"Sure I was," I tell her, grinning down at her, "I had to make sure to get to you first. I'm buddies with just about every other man in town, I'd hate to have to fight one of my friends if they tried to steal my girl."

Chapter Three

Magnolia

Birch calls me his girl like we're dating, or even something more. Maybe I should stop him, but I have to admit, something about it feels right. And I like thinking this smoking hot mountain man might be into me because I'm definitely into him.

The tavern turns out to be the original saloon from Moonshine Ridge's early days as a mining camp. Over the years it's evolved into a dual purpose establishment with a family-friendly restaurant complete with a sign out front that says "only mama cooks it better" taking up most of the building and a bar with a separate entrance facing the parking lot at the back.

"Cedar salvaged some of the original cabinetry," Birch explains, as he gives me a cursory tour.

Cedar is Birch's next youngest brother. He says he has three brothers, all of them still living here in their hometown.

"Well, here abouts, anyway," he grumbles under his breath as the pretty young waitress motions us to a booth in a back corner and brings a couple of menus over.

Birch says yes to the beer she offers to bring him and I order an ice tea.

When the waitress returns with our drinks, we give her our order and I fidget nervously under Birch's dark gaze.

He takes a pull from the cold draft beer he's working on and dabs at the corner of that thick, mountain man beard that my fingers are itching to run through.

Something about Birch makes every part of me feel hot and tingly and I want to touch him so bad it's hard for me to concentrate on anything else.

"So Eliza Manchester is your kin then," he says thoughtfully after awhile, "I'm sure you found all the newspaper articles that got printed about her when she went missing. What made you decide to come all the way up to the ridge on a wild goose chase that was settled over a hundred and fifty years ago?"

"I was just hoping I could find out more about what really happened to her," I explain to Birch over the burgers and chili-cheese fries that our waitress sets down in front of us.

"Thanks, Cami," Birch says to the pretty blonde in a voice so much softer than the one he's been using with me that I can't help but give the girl a more thorough looking over.

She's about my age, so early 20s, blonde hair in a thick braid down her back, and the kind of curves men go crazy over, not like my extra junk in the trunk shape.

Jealousy rears up inside me and I glare after her as she heads back to the kitchen. I should have known better earlier. Birch was just teasing when he said that thing about me being his girl.

Some guys just talk like that, I guess.

Digging into my burger to hide my hurt, I wait for Birch to remember I'm here.

"That girl's giving my brother fits," he says with a chuckle. "If he ever gets his head out of his ass, maybe he'll have a shot at not ending up being the last single McAllister man on the mountain."

"Cami's with Cedar?" I ask between bites of burger and chili cheese fries.

That warmth returns to my body as Birch fixes me under another heavy stare with those deep, coffee-colored eyes of his. There's a pull down in my lower belly and a rush of heat between my legs that has me fidgeting under his gaze.

Half a smirk quirks up one corner of his mouth and I'm distracted by wondering what it'd be like to kiss a man with a beard like that. Something tells me I'd like it. A lot.

"Not yet," he tells me, lowering his voice like we're sharing a secret, "but a man can only fool himself so long and Ash and his wife, Hyacinth, and me? We all see the writing on the wall. It's just a matter of time."

Relief isn't a strong enough word to describe how I feel when I find out that Birch isn't interested in Cami. Maybe he meant what he said about me being his after all. I'm sure hoping to find out.

"Well," he drinks from the beer again, and stares into the distance somewhere just past my shoulder for a long moment,."Rumors have been flying around town for generations," Birch says, speaking slowly and sounding pained, "Grandpa Brodie signed a contract to marry Eliza back in 1871. Records show he paid for her to come to Moonshine Ridge and he collected her at the depot when she got here."

"But they never married," I add, "and even though there's no further mention of her in any of Moonshine Ridge's records, the newspaper in Paradise Point mentions that she'd gone missing and that Brodie was under suspicion for her disappearance."

"My grandfather was exonerated!" Birch's meaty fist hits the table, making everything on it jump and the salt shaker comes down on its side, spilling salt across the table.

"Erm, sorry about that." Birch's cheeks blush pink above the edges of his beard as he dutifully goes about wiping the spilled salt up in one of his huge hands and emptying it on the edge of his empty plate.

"It's just that old gossip never dies around here," he tells me, his voice lowering to a soft purr that I feel all the way into my core. "Grandpa Brodie was one of four men who founded Moonshine Ridge back in the 1870s when it went from being nothing but a mining camp full of men hoping to find their fortune in these mountains, to a proper settlement with a general store, an inn, and postal service. When Eliza disappeared, all eyes turned to him and even though he was eventually cleared of wrongdoing and went on to marry and have a family that's still a pillar of this community today, the McAllister name still has a shadow hanging over it and gossips like Mable Hart just can't give up on the rumor that Brodie had something to do with his fiance's disappearance."

"It's hard living with that kind of smudge on your family name," he says, his eyes dropping off mine for a moment.

"I'm sorry, Birch," I slide my hand across the table and place it over his. My hand is so small compared to his. In fact, all of me is small compared to him. That's not something I'm used to and I like it.

Birch is a giant compared to me. His size makes me feel delicate, but something else about him makes me feel feminine.

His hand turns over and folds around mine. Electricity shoots up my arm and through my body, pebbling my nipples and causing my core to clench.

He's got me fixed in that dark stare of his, looking at me like he wants to devour me, making me wonder if it's possible that he might want me as badly as I want him.

"I'm sorry I can't answer your questions about what

happened to your aunt." His voice so soft and deep it's like soaking in a bath of hot fudge sauce. "But I sure am glad you came looking for her."

Birch

Feels like I've been talking all night and when Cami stops by with the check and let's us know we're welcome to stay as long as we want-- looking around, I see that just about the whole place has cleared out and the crew is already starting to put chairs on top of the tables to clean up for the night. So I guess I have been talking all night.

It's definitely the most I've ever talked about Eliza Manchester with anyone.

Not that it helps Maggie any with her efforts to find the ancestor who's trail stopped here in my home town so long ago, but at least it brought her here to me.

Now I can only hope that she isn't thinking that her kin came to a premature end at the hands of mine. I think it'd kill me if Maggie looked at me and my family like we had that kind of evil in our bloodline.

Not when all I've been able to think about since I first lay eyes on the curvy beauty has been about how I never want her to leave this mountain after today.

I want her here, with me. In my bed and filled with the next generation of McAllisters that will grow up right here on the ridge.

All I gotta do is figure out how to convince her she belongs with me.

"Guess it's time to go, huh?" She laughs lightly as I drop some bills on the table and stand up.

I hate having to let go of Maggie's hand. It's been so comforting holding it all through our conversation and now my palm feels empty without her delicate fingers cradled in mine.

"I'll walk you home," I tell her, waiting for her to gather her things. "Where are you staying?"

"I rented a cottage at the lodge," she tells me, "I haven't even checked in yet. I hope the office is still open."

With a hearty laugh, I take her bag from her and head for the kitchen here at the tavern.

"No worries, I know a guy," I tell her as she takes a few jogging steps to catch up with me.

Instantly I slow my pace to match hers. I love having Maggie by my side and I never want her to feel like she's not my top priority.

"Cam," I call out and get Cami's attention when we get to the waitress station, "get my brother out here, would ya?"

Cami gives me a nod and heads through the doors to the kitchen.

I hear her saying something about me wanting him

out here and I hear my hard-ass brother giving her some shit she probably doesn't deserve. I'll never understand why that girl keeps showing up for work for my asshole little brother, but jobs aren't exactly plentiful here on the mountain, especially not for newcomers to town like Cam.

"Hey big brother!" Cedar comes around the corner, wiping his hands on a towel. His eyes land on Maggie standing next to me and I can't help the low growl that comes out of my throat or the way my arm instinctively goes around her shoulders.

One of Cedar's eyebrows rises on his forehead as he looks from Maggie back up to me, but he doesn't say anything.

"Magnolia says she has a cottage reserved, but I've been talking her ear off since she got off the shuttle this afternoon so she didn't get by the office in time to pick up her key. Any chance you got a spare around here?"

"Hey, Magnolia," my brother grins, extending a hand toward her to shake. "Glad to meet ya, sorry you seem to have gotten stuck with my bonehead brother here."

When Maggie wraps her arm around my waist I swell with pride so much I expect the buttons to rip off my shirt. I love that she seems keen on letting everyone know she's with me.

Cedar heads off to his office behind the kitchen and I hear him saying something to Cami in a terse voice and a minute later she's storming out the door with her purse over her shoulder and her apron in a wad under her arm.

Maggie's head spins to watch the young waitress make her hasty exit and then I feel Maggie's eyes on me. I just shake my head.

"Told ya," I whisper and love the glimpse I get of those full tits as they jiggle with her laughter.

"Here ya go," Cedar says as he hands Maggie a set of keys when he returns from the back room. "Knew I had a set in the office somewhere."

"So what set Cami off just now?" I can't help poking at my little brother.

Cedar rolls his eyes and shakes his head, but I notice the way his gaze focuses on the young waitress still standing in the parking lot beyond the door.

"I don't even know why I keep her on, to be honest," he says, "she's got no waitressing experience and I spend more time having to double check her orders than it takes to cook them."

"She needs the job, bro," I remind him gently, knowing damn well Cedar's not about to fire the little blonde spit fire waitress even if she breaks every dish in the house.

"Yeah. I know. Guess that's why I keep her around," he says with a sigh.

"I thought she was great," Maggie says, sounding both protective of the girl she just barely met, and more than a little like she wants to scold Cedar for acting like an ass.

That's my girl. She's already fitting into the family just fine.

Chapter Four

Magnolia

Birch keeps his arm around me as he escorts me to the cottage I'll be staying in for the week. I like the feel of him against me. He's so big that my shoulder fits under his arm perfectly and I love the weight of his arm draped across my shoulder.

"You think she knows?" I ask as we cut across the parking area where the waitress, Cami, is standing with her phone in her hand. She looks like she's crying and I kinda want to kick Birch's brother's ass for that.

"Who? Cam?" Birch glances over too and we see Cedar poke his head out of the tavern door and yell something at her, gesturing for her to come back inside. "Nah. She doesn't have a clue," he finally says as we continue walking up a little stairway set into the hill behind the lot toward the cottages, "she thinks my brother hates her. Surprised she hasn't told him to kick rocks yet."

"Maybe she likes him too," I muse, snuggling closer to Birch's heat in the crisp mountain evening air.

Birch harumphs somewhere above me.

When we get to the door of cottage number six, Birch stands beside me as if he's keeping watch while I use the set of keys his brother provided to unlock both locks on the door.

The free-standing, one room cottage is positioned on a hill behind the main hotel and tavern, set back in the forest along with the other cottages.

I don't know if Birch is keeping an eye out for bears, or people, but his protective stance is sweet. I like that he's watching over me. It makes me feel safe.

When I get the door open and the light inside turned on, Birch brings my bag in and sets it down on one of the two chairs that are drawn up to a cute little dining set near the kitchenette.

"How long are you planning on staying here?" His voice rumbles through the tiny studio as he pokes his head into the bathroom and checks the closet.

"I rented the cottage for the week," I answer. "Since the shuttle only comes up to Moonshine Ridge once a week, I have to stay till Tuesday."

This is the first time Birch and I have been completely alone together and the king size bed with the frame made of thick, hand-hewn logs taking up most of the space in the small studio cottage is only adding to the sense of intimacy as he finishes his check of my room and comes to stand near me.

Too near.

I'm aching for him to touch me. I want this burly giant of a man to reach out and wrap his arms around me, pull me against his broad chest and let me feel his hard body against mine. I want him to show me that he meant it earlier when he called me his girl.

We may have only known each other for a short time, but already I know Birch is the man I've been waiting for. The first man who's ever made me feel this way, like I belong to him. Like I want to belong to him.

"Sorry I'm not much help," he tells me, his low voice sending goosebumps across my skin.

"Help with what?"

Birch shifts his weight on his feet. It's so cute, like this huge, bearded man could be nervous around me.

"I know you still have questions about your aunt, and maybe I'm not the right person to ask about that," he straightens up and I swear at full height, Birch's head almost collides with the ceiling fan. He takes a deep breath and I see the irritation in his dark eyes.

"There was no way I was going to let Mable Hart and Vera Jones fill you up with their version of things."

His voice vehement. I love that Birch is proud of his family name. That he has a history in this small mountain town that he can trace back to its beginning.

My own family history is a jigsaw puzzle of bits and pieces that don't all fit together. That's why I did the DNA ancestry test to begin with, hoping that maybe I'd find parts of a family that knew where it came from. A family I could belong in.

With a tentative step, I dare to move closer to him. His scent is all fresh laundry, spice, and scents left over from the restaurant that fill my head with ideas of what it would be like share a home with him.

"I think it's great that you have so much pride in your family history," I tell him as my hands stray to his chest without my permission.

He looks down at me and those espresso dark eyes soften. His lips move the edges of his beard higher at the corners and when his arms settle loosely around my shoulders I swear I swoon.

"Sweetheart, I want you to be proud of it too. Because I've been planning on making you part of it since I laid eyes on you."

I'm waiting for the kiss that should follow a statement like that, but instead of feeling Birch's mouth on mine, he untangles his arms from my shoulders and crosses the room in three large steps till he's standing in the doorway.

"There's one more source of information about Brodie McAllister left to consult," he tells me with one hand on the doorknob. "I'll come by tomorrow morning to get ya. Be ready by eight if you want to get something to eat first."

"Lock this door up good after me," he instructs as he steps out into the inky blackness of the forest night. "The Ridge doesn't have much crime, but we get a lot of strangers through this part of town that I can't vouch for. Understand?"

Nodding, I go to the door and bolt the locks after he closes it behind him.

Damn.

Birch

Town isn't all that big, it's an easy walk back to where I left my truck parked behind Ash's sporting goods store.

Heaven knows the chilly spring night air is a big help for calming my overheated blood.

I can't believe I didn't even try to kiss her good night.

Magnolia was standing right there, with her pretty fingers messing with the buttons on my shirt and looking up at me with those pouty lips of her just begging to be kissed.

I'd been looking for excuses all day to touch her, openings to make a move. Then, when I had her in my arms, I blew it.

Maggie showing up has me all kinds of flustered. Between my dick being hard so much of the day and having to get into ancient history that I'd just as soon stay buried forever with my great great great grandpa

Brodie, it's a wonder I can even find my way back to my own cabin.

Truth is, nobody left alive really knows what became of the woman Magnolia came here asking about. Anyone who did know has been gone for a long, long time and they took whatever they knew to the grave with them.

There's always been whispers around town that Brodie took that poor girl into the mountains and left her there.

People like Mable and her toady, Vera, are particularly fond of saying he shot her, hacked her into pieces and tossed them over a cliff for the animals to take care of.

When I was growing up here, the teenagers liked to go up to the lake and scare each other stupid with tales of how the ghost of Eliza Manchester would appear wet and bloated from being drowned in the lake looking for revenge.

I guess every small town has to have an unsolved mystery in its past, I just wish Moonshine Ridge's wasn't tied to my own family name. But my sweet southern blossom still has questions about her aunt Eliza and god help me, I want to help her answer them. Even if it means facing a truth I don't want to believe.

Can't imagine what it would have been like to grow up like Maggie did-- never knowing my daddy or his kin, cousins I never knew about, a mom that never talked about her childhood.

That's something I can always take pride in; growing up in the town where my roots are planted securely under me. Good parents that raised us boys right and set an example of what a loving relationship looks like.

It kills me thinking that Maggie didn't have the same things growing up. I can't wait for her to meet my folks, to bring her into the fold and let the McAllister clan know my baby brother, Ash, isn't the only one who's going to be providing grand babies to spoil soon.

First thing's first; I'll take Maggie to talk to nan tomorrow. If there's anyone left on the ridge that has information about the McAllister family tree that hasn't already been gossiped to death, it'd be my grandmother.

Chapter Five

Magnolia

"Sorry about the coffee," Birch says, leaning low to whisper so his brother doesn't hear. "Tavern's the only place in town to eat besides cooking it yourself. Cedar only started opening for breakfast hours about a year ago."

He tips the heavy, commercial ceramic mug and peers inside with a skeptical look.

"The tavern's really more of a night place," he tells me.

"It's not that bad," I say, trying to keep my laughter quiet. "It's perfectly functional diner level coffee."

Birch grumbles as we prepare to head out. "Ridge needs a good cafe," he mutters. "Someplace with decent java and some good muffins."

After Birch left last night, I tossed and turned most of the night. The bed felt too big for just me, the room was too quiet, sounds from the forest outside kept making me jump and my imagination run wild.

I was disappointed that I hadn't uncovered any more information about the missing branch of my family tree here, but even more disappointed that Birch hadn't stayed the night with me.

He hadn't even tried to kiss me, which over shadowed everything else and left me wondering once again, if I'd been misinterpreting him.

When he came by this morning to walk me down to the tavern for breakfast though, it felt even more like we'd known each other forever. Birch even walked with his arm around me like he wanted the entire town to see us together.

"There's really no where else in town to eat out?" I ask as Birch starts up the truck and we head toward where ever it is that he's taking me today.

"Nope. Used to have a lunch counter at the drug store but that closed down about fifteen years back. It's just Cedar's place now."

It seems odd to me that a town like Moonshine Ridge wouldn't have more than one place to eat. Sure, the town is small, but the road running through it leads to world class hiking and off-road Jeep trails. There's a river rafting business in town and from what I saw online when I looked the area up, the highway ends at a private campground several miles farther up into the mountains that stays busy year round, even in the winter when they have to have guests snow-mobile in.

"Seems like Moonshine Ridge gets enough tourist traffic to sustain another eatery," I mention as we drive past the little general store where the old lady was so interested in my arrival yesterday.

The store is closed now.

"When does the store open?" I ask absently, noticing the clock on Birch's dash reads after ten.

Birch chuckles in that deep rumble that I'm coming to appreciate more and more. With his hulking size and his tendency to scowl from behind that beard, he gives the impression of a man who doesn't laugh much but in less than twenty-four hours that I've known him, I've come to realize that he's really a gentle giant.

At least when it comes to me.

"Store opens when nan opens it," he tells me as we turn up a long, shaded driveway, "and today, nan is opening late because she's going to tell you everything she knows about seven generations of McAllisters in Moonshine Ridge.

"Your grandmother is the woman who owns the general store?"

"Eigthy-one years old, sharp as a tack and refuses to retire."

Birch laughs as he comes around my side of the truck, being a gentleman to open my door, but I didn't wait for him so when he stands ready to close it after me, I'm trapped by his bulk as I climb down from the seat.

Once again, we're chest to chest-- or really more like my boobs to his belly, he's so much taller than me.

The unexpected touch as we collide causes my nipples to pebble. I get another whiff of his manly scent and when I stumble back awkwardly, his hands reach out and grip my upper arms to steady me.

His touch is firm and warm and sends electricity coursing through my blood like its on fire. I tip my head to look up at him and I see the look in his eyes.

I'm ready. I lean in, lifting myself up on my toes, desperate to meet his lips halfway as they lower to mine.

His beard brushes my chin and I feel the heat of his breath against my lips--

"Birch?!"

Birch

My grandmother's voice screeching my name is almost as effective as having a bucket of ice water dumped on me. Not that even a bucket of ice water would do much to tame the raging erection aching to break free from the confines my jeans right now. But it's enough to ruin the moment, that's for damn sure.

"Later." It's little more than a growl that I make that promise to Maggie while we're still eye to eye.

Her pretty lips quirk up in a grin that has me looking forward to doing more than kissing her later.

"Birch, are you comin' in or not? I'm holding the store ya, you know."

While my back is still turned to my nan and Maggie's not looking, I adjust my dick and slam the door of the truck shut.

"Nan, this is my girl, Magnolia. Maggie, this is my grandmother, Alice." I wrap my arm tightly around Maggie's shoulders and steer her toward the old woman giving us a hard glare from the patio of the clapboard house that my brothers and I spent so much time getting yelled at for running through when were growing up.

" 'Girl,' huh," Nan muses as she gives Maggie the standard looking-over. "Can't pretend I didn't see that comin'," she adds with one of Nan's trademark scowls.

"Um," Maggie's head turns to look up at me and then back at Nan. "It's nice to meet you, Alice?"

Nan scoffs and waves a hand. "Might as well call me Nan," she says, "I'm sure that's gonna be about right here in a bit anyway."

I hear Maggie says something low under her breath that I can't make out and when I look down at her she's staring after my grandmother with a confused look on her pretty features as we follow Nan into the house.

"Marcia was going to come over," Nan tells me, "but I guess a goat got out."

Now Maggie's confused look turns up to me.

"There's always a goat out at the Diaz homestead," I explain.

"You two want something to drink?" Nan asks.

"I'll bring out some iced tea," I volunteer, giving Maggie a gentle push toward my nan on her way out to the back patio.

While I pull glasses down from the cupboard and grab the pitcher of sweet tea from the fridge, I think of the memories I have of family dinners with nan and pop on the weekends and summer vacations spent camped out in the tree-house that dad and pop built for us in the pines along the back of the property.

Back when all four of us McAllister boys were thick as thieves and even a bear encounter couldn't get us to sleep inside.

By the time I bring the tray out to the table on the back patio, the women are already deep in conversation.

"What we do know," Nan is saying to a mesmerized Maggie, "is that Brodie married his ex-partner's baby sister just a few months after Eliza went missing. Speculation has always been that he murdered Eliza to get out of the contract he signed for a mail order bride so he could marry Lily instead."

"No one ever found her body," I interject. "No remains, no clothes, no belongings. How do we know she even showed up in town? Maybe the travel manifest is even correct?"

Nan gives me a sympathetic look and sips the tea I pour for her.

"Birch always hated the story," she tells Maggie, "even when he was a boy. I remember having to go pick him up from school when he was in the third grade because he punched Hayle Hart for telling the new kid that the town was founded by a murderer."

"Hayle still deserves punchin'," I grumble.

"So that's all there is to the story then?" Maggie asks. She looks so disappointed and it kills me that she's not getting the answers she's looking. "Brodie killed my aunt so he didn't have to marry her and then everyone just looked the other way because he had clout in the town?"

Nan frowns, her eyes dart from Maggie to me and back and then she leans forward.

"These mountains have more legends than Moonshine Ridge has old ladies to keep them alive, sweetheart," she tells Maggie in a conspiratorial voice.

"People come up here to hunt for Bigfoot, the natives were telling stories about shape-shifters in the forest long before the miners showed up. Ghosts walk the streets of the town and nearly everyone here has a story of their own to tell about it.

"Some people believe Eliza Manchester was bartered off to some kind of creature to buy the new town's protection. I've heard the same story told that it was

Eliza herself that made the choice to go into the woods of her own accord. Point is, people tell tall tales. Especially in places like Moonshine Ridge, where generations have been born and grown with not much else to do and parents try to keep our babies safe from bears and crumbling cliffs by scaring the crap out of them around the fire all winter with stories about werewolves and vengeful ghosts."

Maggie's eyes are wide as she stares at my nan speechlessly. Then looks to me as if I've got anything to add to that.

"Nan, you've never once told me that Eliza Manchester wandered into the woods to marry a Bigfoot," I say.

Nan looks at me.

"Because it's a far-fetched load of hooey and you and your brothers would probably have set off on a hunt to prove it just to clear the family name."

Stupid as it sounds now, I think of myself back when I was nine or ten and I have to admit I might have done exactly what Nan's suggesting. Especially if Cypress had been willing to go along with me.

"Now you two go on and get back to whatever it is you were in the middle of." Nan gets up and shoos at us with a motion of her hands, "I gotta get down to town and open the store. Lord knows if Mable sees the closed sign in the window too long she'll have everyone in town thinking I'm dead by the end of the day."

Chapter Six

Magnolia

"That was...interesting," I say when we're back in the truck and safely out of Alice's hearing.

"Which part?" Birch huffs. "The part where my great great great grandpa still murdered his fiance so he could marry another woman just to piss off his ex-friend? Or the part where he sold her to Sasquatch?"

We both laugh. I totally snort when I do and I can't even be embarrassed about it.

"I don't know why I'm surprised that that's one of the stories. I ran across all kinds of Bigfoot sightings reports when I was looking up Moonshine Ridge."

"Don't forget the werewolves," Birch says. "Apparently rival packs have been roaming the mountains for centuries."

"That I did not hear about," I admit, turning my head to stare at the high, granite peaks that crowd around us in all directions.

Birch makes that harumph noise that I'm starting to find so endearing. "Been running wild in these mountains my whole life, never seen neither," he assures me.

That's comforting. Especially since I'm starting to think Moonshine Ridge might be some place I'd like to call home. With a certain bearded grump who's gone silent beside me as we drive back to the town center where the lodge is.

When we get back to my cottage, Birch walks me to my door just like last night.

That almost kiss back at Alice's house has had me keyed up since Birch's promise that we'd pick up where we left off when we were done at his grandmother's.

The way he made that single word-- *later*-- feel dirty. It soaked through my pores and all the way to my bones and even though I came to Moonshine Ridge hoping to find answers to my family history, finding Birch instead has got me thinking how nice it would be to start making my own family history.

"You gonna be OK here on your own?"

The voice under the beard is his usual gruff tone but there's an added note of sadness to it now.

"You're not coming in?" I hate the high pitch in my voice, my disappointment so obvious.

Birch frowns into the woods behind me, his thick brows knit together and the way the corners of his mouth turn downward has my mind racing with questions.

"Did I do something wrong?" I tack on to my previous question meekly.

"Hell no, you didn't do anything wrong." Birch's eyes come back to mine, a crease denting the space between his eyes.

His hands come up and wrap around my upper arms. Even with him leaning down to face me, I have to tilt my head back so that I can look him in the eyes.

"Sweet girl," even at a whisper, his voice rumbles, "why on earth would you think you did something wrong?"

"It's just that...from the way you were talking...and then earlier when we almost--" My voice falters, I swallow hard and force myself to be brave. To keep my eyes on his and be straight with him.

"I guess I had it in my head that you wanted me like I want you."

Birch's nostrils flare and his throat works visibly with hard swallow.

His hands tighten on my arms.

"I do, Magnolia. I want you like I didn't know was possible for a man to want a woman."

"Then why are you backing off all of a sudden?"

"Ah hell, Maggie," Birch's hands drop off my arms and he straightens back up to his full height. "What would a girl like you want with me? You really want to move your whole life up to some remote mountain town to marry an old grump like me? Spend the rest of your life listening to gossiping old biddies talking about how you married into a family with murder in its background?"

Birch's chest expands with a deep breath and when his eyes fall back to mine I see fire in them.

"Because if I come inside with you, I'm going to make you mine. I'm a weak man with you, Maggie, I won't be able to stop myself. And if we're going that far, we're going all the way. All the way to the altar. All the way to the grave. Because I knew the moment I laid eyes on you that I'd never be able to bring myself to settle for another woman once I tasted you."

OK, I admit, Birch's declaration is a lot. But it doesn't require any thinking on my part.

"That's what I want too Birch." Somehow my voice manages to have some volume to it, because honestly? I'm practically panting now. "Small town gossip is just that, gossip. It doesn't matter how many generations it takes for the stories to get forgotten, I don't even care if the stories are true or not. I want to stay here Birch. With you. I want you to make me yours and I want you to be mine."

For a response, Birch has my back up against the door of the cottage. His lips searing mine in a hard, relentless kiss that has me seeing stars.

It's easy to remember to open my mouth for him, his tongue moving between my lips and then tangling with mine till I'm matching his rhythm.

One of us remembers to unlock the cottage door and

then I'm tumbling inside, wrapped in Birch's strong arms as he moves us closer to the bed.

Birch

Hearing Maggie say she wants me is like pouring gasoline on an already raging fire. My pulse pounds in my own ears and the only thing I'm aware of is the taste of her lips.

Somehow we manage to get to the other side of the cottage door and lock the outside world away from us.

Maggie's hot little tongue is warring with mine now. Her hands are traveling over my chest, working the buttons open on my shirt and the feel of her fingers grazing over my pecs sends new need surging through me.

My cock is straining at my zipper, aching to escape the denim prison of my jeans. It wants Maggie's delicate little hands wrapped around it. Wants to feel her tight sheath stretched over it while she moans my name.

Just the thought is enough to make me feral. I have to break the kiss, rear my head back and groan loud in the small space while I fight to keep some control.

When I look back down, Maggie's got her head tipped up to look at me. Her lips are swollen from my rough kisses and her neck is pink from my beard against her skin.

I need to see that whisker burn pinking her inner thighs. Gotta get my tongue on her sweet pussy and drink my fill of her while she comes on my face.

Pushing her down on the bed that takes up most of the room in here, I finish the job she started of stripping off my shirt.

"You too," I order her, "I need to see you naked, baby."

Without taking her eyes off mine for an instant, Maggie's hands tremble at the buttons on her blouse.

Kneeling down on the floorboards between her knees I reach up and grab the backs of her thighs and pull her roughly to the edge of the bed.

"You nervous, sweetheart?"

I can't help but notice the way her fingers fumble with her undressing for me so I place my hands over hers and hold them still.

Her heart's beating a mile a minute under my touch and I can tell it's from more than just the same adrenaline that has mine beating almost as fast.

"I've never done this before," she whispers with a shy little smile that makes my dick jump.

"Never undressed for a man before?" I ask, slowly unbuttoning her blouse with her hands wrapped around mine now.

The soft material of her yellow blouse parts and falls

away revealing perfect tits over-flowing a lacy white bra beneath.

"Never *been* with a man before," Maggie's voice is strained. She sucks in a sharp breath when I reach into those lacy cups and pull her breast into my mouth.

I can't believe what I'm hearing.

My girl's a virgin.

My tongue rolls over her nipple, sucking till it's extended and puckered tightly when my mouth reluctantly lets it go with a soft pop.

"Never, baby?" I watch the storm in her eyes while I extract her other breast from her bra and rub my thumb across her nipple.

She shakes her head, those dark curls shimmying around her shoulders.

"You sure you want to do this now?"

At that I get an enthusiastic nod and I let out the breath I was holding. I'm not sure how I'd have managed to stop right now if she'd said no.

"Yes, Birch, please," she mewls, pushing her body closer to me, "I need you to do those things you said. Make me yours. That's what I want."

"Lay back, Maggie," I say, giving her a gentle push before peeling her jeans off of those curvy hips and then all the way off.

The sight of her lying there, with her thighs spread wide and nothing on now but a pair of little pink cotton panties that are about soaked through in the middle, it's got my head spinning. I have to reach down and undo my own jeans just to keep my stiff manhood from strangling me.

"You let me know if you need me to slow down," I say.

"Wait," Maggie twists her body to look at me, "what about you? I want to make sure you like it."

"Like it?" Centering the pad of my thumb over the growing wetness of her cotton panties, I press in, feeling the tender spot where I'm dying to get my mouth on. "Baby, I promise you, I already like it."

Before I roll the cute little pink bikinis off of her, I dig my nose in deep and inhale the pure essence of my girl's sweet pussy.

Tugging her panties all the way off, I move between her full thighs and get my first taste of heaven.

Chapter Seven

Magnolia

Birch settles his bulk between my legs and there's no room for self-consciousness as he forces my thighs as wide as they can go.

His mouth lays gentle kisses over my inner thighs. It feels so good but it does nothing to quench the heat raging through my body.

"Please, Birch." I squirm against him, moving my sex to press closer to his mouth, "don't tease."

He chuckles darkly against my mound and I feel his fingers slide into my slit.

My back arches at his touch, a shocked gasp escaping me at the contact.

"Your pussy's so wet baby," he mumbles against me.

Then his mouth is on me, suctioning over my clit at the same time he works one of those thick, blunt fingers inside me.

The sensation has me seeing stars. I'm moving frantically, desperate to get closer to his touch.

"More, Birch," I plead not knowing what more is, just knowing it's what I need.

He slips another finger inside me, working them together to drive me over the edge.

"That's it, Maggie," Birch is saying, "come for me baby. Just let go, honey."

Birch withdraws his fingers but he continues to kiss my sensitive sex while I float back to earth.

"I need to have you now," he says, positioning himself with his hips pushing my thighs wide. "I'll try to go slow for you."

His thick manhood is hard pressed against my mound as he drags himself through my slick folds, making me arch my back at the feel of him. Then he lines the broad head of his dick up with my opening and puts pressure there.

With a light kiss on my lips, he tells me to relax.

"It might hurt some," he warns, "but not for long, I promise."

"Do it, Birch," I whimper, angling up to beg him inside me, "I want to feel you inside me, please."

"Damn, baby, when you say things like that you make it hard to be gentle."

He enters me slowly, inch by inch. I can feel the effort of his restraint in the tension of his back and shoulders. His face is screwed into a mask of concentration as he fills me up completely.

There's just a slight stinging sensation as he tears through my virginity but then I feel so warm and full that I can't stand another second without moving.

"Baby, I need to move now," he chokes out.

"Yes, Birch, please, me too," I answer as he pulls back, leaving me feeling empty and hungry for him to fill me again.

My body follows his instinctively and then Birch thrusts forward again, fast and forceful, pushing into me and then sliding back again until I manage to find the rhythm and move with him.

And then that feeling is building inside me again, only this time it's better, stronger, threatening to break me apart and I can't stop it even if I tried.

"Yeah, Maggie, that's it baby, come on my cock like a good girl." Birch is growling into my ear, his hips continuing to slam into me where our bodies are joined.

Then I hear a strangled groan from him as I fall apart again, every muscle in my body tenses and releases and just when I think it's over, I hear Birch let loose a torrent of curse words.

His thrusts come faster and then he goes rigid, pressed to the hilt inside of my body as he let's go with a deep grunt. I feel him filling me with his release before collapsing against me.

Birch

. . .

I knew it'd be like that. I knew Maggie's curvy little body was going to be like coming home and now that I've had her I know I'll never get enough.

It kills me when our bodies part, making me want to get back inside her as soon as possible but I know my girl is going to need some time. So I roll off of her and pull her into my arms.

After a few minutes of silence I can feel her body tense and I know she's thinking about things we need to get clear between us.

"Tell me what you're thinking, baby," I say softly against her cheek.

"Nothing," she squirms a bit, burrowing against my chest.

I'm about to call bullshit but then she tells me.

"Did you mean it?" Her head turns to look back at me and I have to move so I can face her.

"Mean what?" I let her roll over so she's on her side, facing me with her head propped up on her hand but I can't stand not having her warmth pressed against me so I reach out and pull her tight to me again.

"About being yours?" Her voice has gone small as she snuggles into my shoulder now and my arm tightens around her soft body. "What you said about going to the altar-- do you want that with me, Birch? Or were you just trying to get laid?"

I try not to scoff too hard. I guess I can see how she might be surprised at how fast things are moving, but Maggie's my everything, and I tell her so.

"Sweet Magnolia blossom," I turn so she can look me in the eye when I tell her. "I'd marry you today if I thought I could get away with it."

She's grinning at me, those pretty blue eyes of hers shining like the sun hitting the lake at mid-day.

"I knew you were the one for me the moment I saw you," I tell her. "You've heard my whole family story now and you still want to be with me. You are the woman I want in my home, in my bed, filled with my babies and growing old beside me, baby."

"Oh Birch!"

Now I see tears rimming her pretty eyes, but from the way she's throwing her arms around my neck and kissing me, I'm guessing they aren't the kind of tears I need to be kissing away.

"I love you, Birch." She whispers it like she's scared to tell me but hearing it makes me feel like I need to be down at the tavern buying a round to celebrate.

"I love you too, Maggie," I tell her. It's the easiest thing I've ever said, because it's the God's honest truth.

This time when she kisses me, she lingers, her tongue sweet and curious as it sneaks past my lips.

Her bare breasts are pressed against my chest and my dick's hard for her again already.

Maggie's little hand slides down between us and

wraps around my girth and she looks back up at me with a wicked little smile.

"You sure you're ready for round two, sweetheart?" I tease her as I lay her back into the pillows.

"Definitely," she tells me, "but this time I want to be on top."

Chapter Eight

Magnolia

We made love all afternoon and only ventured out when we realized we skipped lunch and dinner. Fortunately, the bar of the tavern stays open late and Birch was able to get us something to eat before the kitchen shut down for good.

He ran out to pick up food while I showered and now we're sitting at the little table in the cottage's kitchenette talking about big plans.

"First we get you a ring," he tells me. "Tomorrow, we'll head down to Slow River and hit every jewelry store they have until you find what you want. Then we introduce you to the whole clan, you already met Cedar and Nan, you'll love the folks and Ash and his wife aren't hard to get along with but Cypress, well let's just say, you already promised to marry me. No backsies."

Birch has been filling me in on the parts of his

family tree that didn't get covered in my search for the true story of Eliza Manchester.

Apparently, his oldest brother, Cypress, holds the family title for "real" mountain man-- living somewhere up in the wilderness outside of town with a herd of alpacas and no phone or internet.

Ash and his wife Hyacinth are the couple I saw in the sporting goods store when I first arrived in town and, of course, grumpy Cedar who owns the tavern and the lodge. Birch tells me he's getting everyone together at his parents' place for a family dinner so we can make our big announcement.

While we talk about me moving in with him, I scroll through my email on my phone.

"Your boss is just going to have to get over it," Birch grumbles when I point out that I should give two weeks notice at the donut shop where I've been working. "You're not working for another two weeks for -- what's wrong? Maggie? Is everything OK?"

Birch

After an afternoon spent exhausting ourselves while I get to know every curve and crease of Maggie's sweet body, I shamelessly played the family card to get the night crew at the tavern's bar to hook us up with some grub.

I'm chattering away between bites, eager to have Maggie meet the entire family and get her moved in with me as soon as we make our engagement official--but I'm not telling her my plan for that.

While we talk and eat, Maggie looks through her phone. I know she's going to have to tell her roommates that she's moving out and her job is just going to have to suck it up because she's not going back to work for two lousy weeks at some minimum wage paying donut shop.

I see her face go pale and she's staring at the small screen like she's seen a ghost.

"Maggie, what's wrong?"

She's got me worried and whatever the problem is, I'm ready to take care of it.

"It's a new notification from the DNA test place," she tells me.

Moving close to her, I put a hand on her thigh, eager to hear more.

"I have a new relative in my family tree."

She sounds confused and she holds the phone up so I can see. It's a just a bunch of lines and names I don't know in a spread out flow chart.

"Right there," she points, "Violet Turner."

"Huh," I grunt. "Cousin, eh?"

Maggie's finger traces back up through the chart. My eyes follow it to the name Clara Turner several levels up.

"That can't be," Maggie mutters. "The only common relative Violet and I have is here. Except this Clara Turner on my records is Eliza Manchester. See?"

Maggie opens an image on her phone and shows me what looks like the same chart without the part that drops down to Violet. Sure enough, up at the top, there's Eliza's name.

"Can you contact this Violet person?" I ask.

"Already on it," Maggie says.

Her fingers fly over her screen for a few minutes and then she puts it down again and looks over at me, her hand reaching to hold mine.

"Maybe Eliza Manchester didn't get sacrificed to a Bigfoot after all," she says.

I admit, I'm just as curious about this new cousin of Maggie's as she is and if it solves the mystery of whatever happened between Eliza and my great, great, great, grandfather a hundred and fifty years ago or so? All the better. But all I really care about is the woman with her tiny hand wrapped in mine, looking at me like with love in her eyes and making me feel like a king.

"Whatever we find out, isn't going to change my mind about starting a new branch of the McAllister family tree with you, baby," I tell her. "As soon as possible."

Epilogue

Epilogue 1
A Few Months Later
Maggie

I'm so excited! Birch and I are planning our wedding for the end of the summer and I have a brand new cousin slash best friend to be my maid of honor.

Violet turned out to be directly descended from the one and only Eliza Manchester all right. We emailed back and forth for a few days and since Violet grew up down in Slow River, it was easy for us to get together in person.

The best part? Violet has the diary that Eliza kept all those years ago containing the first hand account of her story.

Turns out, Brodie McAllister was distraught to learn his mail order bride had been contracted to marry him against her will. Her parents didn't approve of the man she loved so her father petitioned to find her a husband out west.

When Brodie found out, he had her write to her true love and arranged for him to come meet up with her. Brodie helped her with a new identity and the reason no one ever knew what happened to her is because Eliza Manchester really did disappear right here in Moonshine Ridge.

But Clara Manning married Elijah Turner in a courthouse ceremony down in Slow River with just the justice's wife and Brodie McAllister signing as witnesses on their marriage license.

What a wild story to add to the McAllister family history. It spread like wild fire through town as soon as Violet brought a scanned version of her great great great great grandmother's diary to be included in Mable's museum of local history.

Of course, local lore and ghost stories being what they are, there are new versions of the same old story floating around town already.

But Birch and I aren't worried about the gossip surrounding the McAllister name and we plan on making sure our baby grows up to be just as proud of his or her heritage here in in Moonshine Ridge as the rest of the family is.

I only just found out that I'm pregnant so I have the

wedding timed just right, I probably won't even be showing yet.

Now, if I can just all three of the McAllister men to agree to come to the wedding; Ash and Hyacinth have agreed to be in the wedding and Cedar and Cami are also in-- now that they've finally worked their shit out-- but getting Cypress off his mountain is hard enough for family dinners. It'll be a miracle if I can get him to show up, let alone be in the wedding party.

As long as Birch is waiting for me at the altar though? I don't care if it's just us and the preacher in the pouring rain. It'll be the perfect day.

Epilogue

Epilogue 2
Five Years Later
Birch

Waking up with my wife's hot little mouth sliding down my shaft is always a treat. I'm awake long before I open my eyes, just enjoying the sensation of her soft hand gripping my cock by the root while her tongue flicks over the head, lapping up the drops of precum leaking from the tip.

I know as soon as I lift my head up and look down at Maggie with her mouth full of my dick, I'll either explode down her throat or flip her over and have her on all fours while I fill her up with my seed.

The feel of Maggie's mouth and hands on me is just

one of those things I never get enough of, even after all these years together and the two beautiful babies she's given me, she's still the sexiest woman I've ever seen.

This morning is no exception. Sure enough, when I pull the covers back and get a look at her nestled between my legs with those big blue eyes looking up at me and her hand wrapped around my hard length, I can feel my balls tighten and my dick surges in her grip.

"Good morning," Maggie coos from between my thighs, "I thought you were sleeping in today?"

"You know darn well I can't sleep in with you touching me like that, woman."

She shrugs and drags her tongue down the underside of my shaft and I'm about two seconds from coating her sweet face with my cum.

"Get up here," I growl at her, pulling her on top of me, "I want to come inside your little pussy."

Maggie doesn't hesitate, she impales herself on my cock and rides me just the way she knows how.

Soon we're both panting and all it takes is my thumb pressed against her clit and she's going off like a rocket, her body tensing and her sweet channel sucking me deeper and milking my dick till I can't stop myself.

I come with a groan, emptying my balls deep in my wife's womb.

Maggie collapses and cuddles on my chest and I stroke her dark curls thinking about how glad I am that she talked me into taking the day off. It's nice to have a trustworthy manager down at the sawmill now so I can spend more time home with my family.

"Baby, you keep riding me like that and we're gonna have to start that addition to the house."

We've been talking about it. Another baby. Maybe two more before we call it quits. I already have the plans drawn up for the addition of two more rooms and an extra bathroom on the back of the house. Not that I'm opposed to doubling the kids up-- me and my brothers shared rooms all the way up till the day we left home-- but Maggie says girls need their own space and since we have the room and the means, I'm all for spoiling all my girls rotten.

Maggie's sleepy little voice is soft against me where her fingers are drawing little circle in the hair on my chest.

"You should hire a crew now," she says. "You only have six more months to get it done."

"Wait, what?" I can't believe what I'm hearing, "Six months? You're already three months in?"

I have her rolled over and pinned under me and she's giggling between kisses because my beard tickles her.

"I know! I thought my cycle was off because I just stopped the birth control but I went to see the doctor and sure enough-- three months already."

"Is this why you wanted me to take a day off?"

"No," Maggie flutters her eye lashes and gives me one of those naughty little smiles I like so much, "I thought the girls could spend the day with grandma and grandpa and I could spend the day chasing my husband through the house naked."

"You know you don't have to chase me, baby, I'm never gonna run from you."

Next in the McAllister Men of Moonshine Ridge
Cedar

"Chamomile, like the tea," she says. But nothing about this sassy bundle of curves is like a calming mug of tea.

Cami owned my heart from the moment she came into the tavern I run here in Moonshine Ridge looking for a job. Too bad she's only staying till the end of the summer.

She thinks I'm just her grumpy boss, an old man that needs a shave and a lesson in manners. The truth is I lose my mind every time I catch a whiff of her sweet scent.

I know I don't have a chance in hell with my pretty young employee, but when she tells me she's quitting her job so I won't have to put up with her any more? That's when I know I have to set her straight.

Chamomile is mine, plain and simple and I'm not about to let her get away .

Surrender to the Mountain Man

The McAllister Men of Moonshine Ridge

About

Cedar McAllister

"Chamomile, like the tea," she says. But nothing about this sassy bundle of curves is like a calming mug of tea.

Cami owned my heart from the moment she came into the tavern I run here in Moonshine Ridge looking for a job. Too bad she's only staying till the end of the summer.

She thinks I'm just her grumpy boss, an old man that needs a shave and a lesson in manners. The truth is I lose my mind every time I catch a whiff of her sweet scent.

I know I don't have a chance in hell with my pretty young employee so I keep my distance.

Until a drunk in the bar puts his hands on her and I make it clear how I really feel.

Now that my secret is out, nothing can stop me from making Cami mine.

Rocklyn Ryder

Welcome to Moonshine Ridge and the rugged wilderness surrounding the remote mountain community where the history is long, the local lore is deep, and the men are as wild as the mountains they come from.

Protective, possessive, totally obsessed; the men of Moonshine Ridge will do anything necessary to claim the women they love and give her the happily ever after she deserves.

The Moonshine Ridge books contain a lot of insta love, some swearing, some steamy scenes, zero cheating, and a lot of swoon-worthy happy endings.

Cedar and Chamomile

Surrender to the Mountain Man
The McAllister Men of Moonshine Ridge book 3
by
Rocklyn Ryder

Chapter One

Chamomile

There's less to Moonshine Ridge than I expected. It's not much more than what you see along the highway as the shuttle comes into town.

"Highway" isn't exactly what I would call the road that winds from the foothill town of Keller's Ferry up the steep mountain grade to the end of the line in front of the Moonshine Ridge General Store where I'm standing now.

The main bus line ends at the depot in Keller's Ferry along with the four-lane road. I had to transfer to a smaller shuttle van to get here.

There's a hot springs resort and a lake with world class fishing at the end of the road, a ski resort, Jeep trails, and apparently the thick forests covering the mountain terrain beyond town here are a hot bed of Bigfoot encounters.

I don't know-- I just figured Moonshine Ridge would

be bigger. The place has to get a lot of tourist traffic, right?

Turning a slow three-sixty and getting a good look at the little town around me, I can almost hear Moonshine Ridge itself answering, "as if."

Inside the general store there's a woman who looks to be in her late seventies or early eighties spying on me from behind the single cash register at the counter. She looks like the type of woman who probably knows everyone and everything that's going on in town.

Pushing through the heavy front door with the big plate glass center, I make my way inside Moonshine Ridge's general store.

It's not very big. The gas station mini market where I grew up was bigger than this entire store but when I look around, I can see it has a little bit of everything an average household needs.

There's a small section of fresh produce at the front of the store; apples and lemons and potatoes fill baskets set on long tables. A small refrigerated section holds an assortment of greens, carrots, summer squash and peppers next to cold cases with an adequate supply of dairy products, eggs, and soda pop.

Rows of dry goods run perpendicular to the cold cases, lined with everything from soups and potato chips to toiletries to motor oil.

The single check-out counter is to my right as I come through the front door and the woman behind it gives me a hard looking over but not a smile.

"Hi," I say brightly, moving closer to her and standing across the counter from her. "I'm new in town--"

"No shit," the woman says bluntly, cutting me off.

OooKay then. It takes me a second to recover from my shock.

"I-I was wondering if you might be hiring for the summer?" I ask, my confidence shaken.

The woman narrows her eyes at me and turns to scan the vacant aisles of the store before fixing me in another judgmental stare.

"Because the place is bustling and you figure I can't handle the crowds on my own?"

Just when my first interaction with the locals has me feeling like I'd be better off hiking all the way back down to Keller's Ferry and forgetting I ever heard of Moonshine Ridge, the old woman's face softens into a wide smile accompanied by what I'm pretty sure is a genuine laugh.

"Sweetheart," she takes a step back and climbs up on a stool, "it's a small town. Folks here are decent and we welcome most strangers. You don't have to try so hard."

"Um, OK, thanks," I do my best to return the smile she's giving me now. "Does that mean you need help at the store?"

"Heavens no," she tells me, waving a hand at me, "but you might try down at the tavern--" She lowers her head and gives me another discerning gaze. "You old enough to serve liquor in this state?"

"Twenty-two." I nod.

She nods with me. "Tavern, then. Probably the best shot you have at finding work that doesn't require a chain saw or a truck in this town."

She turns on the stool and points at the wall behind her.

"Tell him Alice sent you," she tells me. "May or may not do you any good."

With a laugh, I say thank you to Alice and head back down the street toward the building a block away that says "Tavern and Lodging" on a big sign out front.

There's a hand-painted sandwich board sign on the sidewalk near the front door that says "Only mama makes it better," with a picture of a hamburger, fries, and shake that looks like it came straight off a poster from a 1950's diner.

Inside, I find myself standing in front of a long diner counter that separates the dining room from the kitchen. Booths line the outer walls around the perimeter of the building, under big windows that look out onto the main street.

A small cabinet sits against the wall just inside the door leading in from the vestibule and there's a stack of laminated menus on it with a chart of the dining room.

"Go ahead and grab a menu, just sit anywhere," a woman's voice calls out from somewhere behind the window into the kitchen, "we'll find ya."

"Um, actually, I was hoping to talk to someone about a job?" I lean over the diner counter between the stools and call back toward the voice that was just talking to me. "Um, Alice sent me?"

Hopefully, Alice's name is worth some magic in this place.

Cedar

"Need you out front, boss," Mil hollers from the doorway of my office.

Of course, by the time I look up to ask her what for, she's already gone back to the kitchen.

"What did you need, Mil?" I ask my day shift cook, poking my head through the kitchen door.

Mildred looks up at me from the grill where she has burger patties lined up, some already flipped with cheese melting over them, some she just laid down.

Order slips are lined up above her and Josh is on the other side of her, making quick work of assembly and plating orders.

"Not me," Mil answers, waving a spatula in the general direction of the lobby, "her."

That's about all I'm going to get from Mildred. She's a godsend around the kitchen here at the tavern, but she's not much for details.

Heading out to the front counter, I scan the lobby for the "her" that Mil's talking about and when I see her, I know there's nothing she could ask me for that I won't say yes to.

The girl in question is standing near the hostess station giving her full concentration to the bulletin board we have on the wall by the door where everyone on the ridge posts up their odd jobs or rooms for rent and pets for adoption.

I don't interrupt for a long moment. I just stand here and drink her in. Committing everything about her to memory.

She's young, for sure, but she's no teenager. With her long blonde hair coiled down her back in a single, thick braid and a sweet hour glass figure that looks like it has an extra twenty minutes thrown in for good measure.

She's wearing those stretchy yoga pants that show off thick thighs and shapely legs all the way down to a pair of ankle high hiking boots and a flannel shirt in a feminine pink plaid with shirt tails that don't quite cover the swell of her full hips and ass.

When my hardening dick presses uncomfortably against the zipper of my jeans, I know I've been staring too long. Caught up in thoughts that are racing in directions I've got no business going in.

Whoever this golden-haired angel is, I plan on making her mine.

"Mil said you were looking for me?" I clear my throat and get her attention, my voice coming out loud and harsher than I mean it to from trying to make sure she

Surrender to the Mountain Man

can't tell she has me shaking with the restraint it takes not pull her into my arms.

She startles slightly and when she looks up at me from across the small space between us, sea green eyes widen before she seems to collect herself and approach the counter.

"Sorry," she says, "the woman in the kitchen just told me to wait here. I was hoping you might be hiring? Alice told me to check here."

As soon as I hear Alice's name I groan, causing my newest waitress to shift her weight between her feet and those gorgeous green eyes to fall to the floor.

Shit, I made her uncomfortable. She's probably thinking that means I'm not interested. She's got no idea just how interested I am.

This girl has no idea what a meddling old gossip my grandmother is. She's just an innocent bystander looking for a job.

"Sorry," I mutter. "Do you have any experience? Waitressing? Cooking? Bartending? How old are you? Can you serve liquor?"

"Twenty-two," she tells me with confidence, "and no, sir, I don't have any kind of food service experience...but I learn fast."

That's good to hear, because I already have a list of things I plan to teach her.

First thing's first, I have to drag my mind out of the gutter and stop imagining her spread out on my bed at home with her perfect tits in my hands and her legs wrapped around my neck.

Normally I'd start her out in the kitchen with Mil and let her do some hostessing while she learns the ropes, but we do need the extra help.

"OK, have a seat and I'll bring the paperwork over."

The way her eyes light up makes me feel like a king and I can't wait to find more ways to get her to look at me like that.

She heads for the empty booth by the window when I motion in that direction and then I head back to my office to grab the paperwork-- and adjust my dick.

Chapter Two

Chamomile

The way he groaned when I said Alice's name had me thinking I didn't have a chance at getting a job here.

That would have sucked. I mean, yeah, I need a job for the summer and all but if I'm being completely honest? The guy who's apparently my new boss is just plain smoking hot.

When I first turned and saw him, I felt a tingle go all the way through me.

He's way over six feet tall, with dark hair cropped in that sexy short but longer on top style and a beard that's full and thick but neatly trimmed. And the way his t-shirt looked like it was being pushed to its limits where it was stretched around those bulging biceps?

Just thinking about it while I sit in the booth waiting for him to come back has me flushed and squirming on the vinyl seat cushion.

"OK--"

Oh, and that voice! It's deep and rumbly in a way that vibrates through me. I bet it can shake the rafters when he yells and I bet it's dark and bossy when he's talking dirty in the bedroom.

He slips into the seat on the other side of the booth from me with some paperwork in his hands just in time to catch my blushing furiously for getting caught thinking about him that way.

"So let's back up a bit first, what's your name?"

"Chamomile, like the tea," I tell him, forcing myself to look him in the eye even though it makes me feel like he can read my thoughts.

A smile curves his lips and that just makes me focus on his mouth. Full lips, a flash of straight, white teeth. Now I'm thinking about kissing him. What would it be like? Would he be--

"Nice to meet you, Chamomile," he interrupts my totally inappropriate day dreaming, "I'm Cedar McAllister. I own both the tavern and the lodge. I do the cooking in the evenings and you met Mildred already, she cooks the day shifts."

He's filling out paperwork, asking me for the information he needs as he goes.

"So you don't have any experience in food service at all?"

That gorgeous face looks up at me, his eyebrows furrowed, the pen in his hand tapping lightly against the tabletop.

Surrender to the Mountain Man

Is he changing his mind?

Shaking my head, I fiddle with my hands in my lap and bounce my knee nervously.

"No," I admit again, "but I'm a hard worker, I like people, and I have worked retail before. I don't know if that helps?"

His eyes are already a dark brown but now they darken. The smile is gone, replaced by a grim sort of expression like he's not happy with my answer.

"What hours are you available?" He asks. Am I imagining it? Or does he sound a little irritated? "Do you have-- obligations-- at home?"

He clears his throat lightly, "Do you have a husband? Boyfriend? Children? Anyone who needs you home certain days or hours?"

He's all business now, his eyes focused on the paperwork in front of him and if I thought there was some hint of interest in his eyes earlier, it's gone now.

"No," I tell him honestly. "But I'm only in Moonshine Ridge for the summer," I add. His face goes all frowny when I say that and I worry it's going to be a deal breaker.

"So you're not planning on staying here long term?"

"Not really, no."

He heaves a sigh that makes him sound tired, writes down a few more things on the papers and pushes them across the table toward me.

"OK, you need to fill this out here, and sign here and here. I'll just go make copies of your documents and then I'll show you around. I already have the schedule made out till Sunday, but I'll add a couple of shifts over the next few days so you can get started."

He slides his bulk out of the booth and heads back through the hallway that leads to the kitchen.

I fill in the few things I need to, read everything over, and sign where he told me to.

"Thanks for coming by today, Chamomile," his deep voice comes from just beside me as he returns to the table and stands next to the bench seat where I'm sitting.

"Cami," I tell him, trying to slide out of the booth only to find myself eye level with his-- um, yeah.

Nice belt buckle, I think. But I'm not exactly looking at his belt buckle.

Cedar takes a step backwards, giving me space to get out of the booth and on to my feet but when I do, I'm still standing close enough to him that I can smell his cologne. Something that suits him well. I inhale, trying not to be obvious. Spice and woodsy and a hint of something fresh like citrus maybe.

Definitely a scent that I will associate with Cedar from now until forever.

"You can start tomorrow at four. That's when I take over the kitchen so you'll be working under me while you learn the ropes."

I never thought I was the kinky type, but if working under him comes with ropes, I'm in.

"Cami?"

"Huh? Oh, tomorrow. Got it. Four o'clock. Ropes." I am such a huge dork. I feel my face heat as soon as I say ropes. It totally sounds dirty and not at all like what he meant.

"Molly will be on shift tomorrow so she can train you."

"Molly. Right." I repeat like I only speak broken parrot.

I'm not sure if I'm waiting for him to shake my hand or if he's waiting for me to leave, but neither of us does anything while we stand there longer than feels comfortable.

"Then I guess I'll see you tomorrow," I finally mumble, ducking away from the heat radiating off his broad chest and making a run for the door and air that doesn't smell like him.

Cedar

This is a mistake. There's a voice inside my head screaming it at me the whole time I'm filling out her tax papers, trying to keep my dick down and my mind focused.

Having Cami around at work is going to be a challenge.

At least she answers no to a husband or a boyfriend. That has me relaxing but only by a little bit because the next thing she says is that she's only staying on the ridge for the summer.

The news has me panicking, silently calculating how long I have with her. How long do I have to convince her to make Moonshine Ridge her permanent home? To make *me* her home?

Fuck. For all I know she's going back to college somewhere at the end of the summer. I might not be able to convince her to stay here with me.

A girl like Chamomile isn't going to want to stay in a place like Moonshine Ridge forever and she sure as hell doesn't want to get tied down to some overworked old man like me.

Twenty-two years old. She's a decade younger than me. Still figuring out what life is all about and what she wants from it.

We'll both be better off if I steer clear of her.

By the time Cami's paperwork is complete and I've got her penciled in for tomorrow's evening shift, I'm convinced that no matter how bad I want her, she's off limits.

Especially now that she's officially an employee.

When Cami rushes out the front door after assuring me she'll be back tomorrow afternoon, I let out a breath that I swear I've been holding since I first saw her.

"Ya hired her, didn't ya?" Mil's voice calling out from the kitchen pulls me back to reality.

"We need the help," I remind her as I check on the

dining room to make sure Patty has the place covered on her own.

"We need experienced help," Mil tells me, "not pretty help."

Patty gives me a wave from across the room where she's setting a bottle of hot sauce on the table in front of Howard Smalls.

Satisfied that she doesn't need my help, I start making my way back to the office, knowing Mildred's onto me.

That only makes me more determined to keep my hands to myself. And if I'm going to see Cami every day and not act on my attraction to her, I'm sure my hands will be very busy with myself.

Chapter Three

Chamomile

Crash!

A plate goes crashing to the ground before I can get it in the bin.

Three weeks working at the tavern and I'm still dropping stuff.

Josh rushes in with the broom and dust pan and I hear Cedar's growl from behind me where he just passed by on his way back to the kitchen.

He barely even talks to me anymore. Just growls when I do something wrong or rolls his eyes if I ask a question I should know the answer to by now.

The thing is, it seems like I'm always screwing up at work. At least, it probably seems that way to Cedar. Because it's only when he's around that I drop stuff. Or get orders wrong.

My first week on the job, he was so kind. He

patiently explained every detail of the business and walked me through every duty I'd need to perform while working here.

We worked late nights closing together and after the customers had left and we locked the doors, Cedar would make us something to eat and we'd talk while we cleaned up.

He seemed interested in getting to know me at first, he asked about where I'm from and where I'm going next and he told me all about his family history here and how his great great great grandfather was one of the men who founded the town in the 1800s.

I met his brother, Ash and Ash's pretty wife, Hyacinth. They run the sporting goods store up the block and sometimes they come in for lunch. They got married a last summer after knowing each other for three days and Hy is expecting their first baby in just a few weeks.

When I see them together it's so hard not to want that for myself. A family, a husband that's so devoted to me he doesn't even notice anyone else.

Unfortunately, I find myself imagining it with Cedar. And despite those first few days when we were friends and every so often, I even got the impression that maybe he saw me the way I see him, lately he's made it very clear that I misread him.

It doesn't help that he only schedules me to work the same shifts as him. It'd be easier working breakfasts when he's not here, but I understand that lunch and dinner are when we're busiest, with not just the main dining room open but the bar in back as well.

Nights like tonight, when I'm covering both, at least keep me busy enough that I don't have to be around Cedar much. And the tips are good.

The bell on the door chimes and I see Cedar's older brother, Birch walk in with a pretty brunette. I've met Birch a few times, he runs the sawmill that was established by Brodie McAllister when the town's gold mining boom stopped booming. Birch makes Cedar look civilized, with his hulking frame, wild beard and permanent scowl.

But not this afternoon. I notice my boss's brother is smiling every time he looks at the girl he's brought in with him.

"Grab a seat, guys," I tell them, motioning over to a row of booths on the far wall while I grab some menus for them.

Every time I stop by Birch and Maggie's table for the rest of the evening, they're deep in conversation, with eyes only for each other.

When I drop by with the check, their hands are entwined on the table top between them and my heart clenches.

On my way into the kitchen to grab orders for the guys in the bar, I catch sight of Cedar. He's so handsome, standing over the grill with his black apron on and another one of his T-shirts that fit tight across his arms and chest, showing me all the muscles my fingers are itching to touch.

His bread is full but not like his brothers', Cedar keeps his trimmed and his hair shorter. His shoulders are broad and his torso narrows in that sexy V-shape that makes my mouth water, thinking about what he'd look like without a shirt on. Or maybe even without anything on.

When I grab the orders, he looks up at me with the same scowl I've come to expect but then it softens a tad when his eyes focus on me. I feel like he's really looking at me for the first time in forever.

It has my pulse kicking up and that tugging feeling tightens my lower belly. I fight to keep my breathing even.

"Birch wants you out front," I tell him as I head out of the kitchen to deliver chili cheese fries to the guys in the bar.

"Cam!" Cedar's voice booms through the doors as they swing shut, "I need to see you after closing, so don't take off."

Shit. This is it. I'm getting fired for sure.

Surrender to the Mountain Man

Cedar

Something's gotta give.

If I don't put a stop to the way things are going now, Cami's going to break every dish in the house. Mildred and Patty say it's me. That I'm such a damn jerk whenever Cami's around that I make her nervous.

Apparently she's a model employee when I'm not here.

Which isn't often. I admit to not wanting her working when I'm not on shift with her. I want to keep an eye on her.

I pretend it's just because she's new and doesn't have experience with serving, that'd I do the same thing with any new waitress. But that's a damn lie.

I want to see her. I want to smell her. I want to hear her voice every day. And I want to make damn sure that none of the local single men think she's up for grabs.

That's a dick move and I admit it. It's not fair of me to play king cock block if I'm not going to claim her for myself but I'll be damned if I'm going to watch any of the assholes around Moonshine Ridge make a move on my girl.

Even if she's not mine.

I've tried. I have fucking tried. I tried staying casual and being friendly but after a week of talking and laughing together, getting to know Cam while we worked together and I couldn't handle it. I knew that being just friends was never going to be enough for me.

So I backed off. Started avoiding being alone with her while we worked together. Listened to her break dishes and started double checking tickets when she started getting orders wrong.

But that hasn't cut down on my cold showers or jacking off three times a day like I was a damn teenager again. If anything, she's only gotten deeper into my head.

I go to sleep pissed that she isn't in my bed. I wake up pissed that she's isn't beside me. I hate that my house isn't full of the sound of her and the scent of her and I hate that every time she sees me now, she runs the other way.

When I came in to take over the kitchen this afternoon, I caught one look at Chamomile, with her thick blonde hair in that single braid down her back, and the short denim skirt and soft t-shirt in the feminine cut under the navy blue apron my staff all wear and my mind was made up.

This stops now. Tonight.

The sound of another dish hitting the floor echoes through the back to the kitchen and I peer through the pick-up window to where Josh is quickly handling the clean-up while Cami sneaks a worried look in my direction.

My eyes catch hers and all I can do is let out a low growl. It feels like my blood is on fire every time those wide green eyes are on mine and it only makes it harder to get through the rest of the night.

Moments later, she whirls through the kitchen, picking up orders that are headed for the bar and avoiding eye contact. She's already through the doors before she tells me my brother needs me up front and I have to yell after her that I expect to see her after closing.

I don't get an acknowledgment, but I see her shoulders tense as she makes her way through the hallway that connects the bar to the kitchen.

My first instinct is to chase after her, pull her into my chest and wrap my arms around her. I want her to know I'm not mad at her, she hasn't done anything wrong, she's perfect in every way-- fuck the broken dishes. I can replace dishes all day long if it means she'd be mine.

Bedding down the impulse, I let her do her job while I head out to the front counter to see what Birch wants.

Out front, I bullshit with my older brother and take note of the curvy little thing he's got tucked under his arm tonight.

He gives me a low growl when he sees me looking and I can't hide my smirk, but I do hide the pain that stabs my chest as jealousy flares.

Our baby brother, Ash, came back from a fishing trip last summer with a woman that has him wrapped around her finger. They got married in a hot minute and now I can't show up for family dinner on Sunday nights at our folks' house without hearing about the grandbaby count down.

I don't know where this girl, Maggie, came from, but from the way she and my brother are looking at each other, it's obvious it's not going to be long till we're adding another chair to the family table.

At least Cypress won't beat me to the altar. That rough bastard living up there on his mountain with his goats is never going to find a woman.

When I head into my office to grab a set of keys for Maggie's cottage, Cami comes storming through the hallway from the bar like she's on fire.

"I'm out of here," she tells me in a voice that's a whole lot of mad but shaking with the verge of tears. She pulls off her apron and wads it under her arm in a ball, grabbing her purse from the hook inside my office door before spinning on her heels.

"I told you I needed to talk to you after closing, don't go anywhere, I'll be right out."

My voice is louder and rougher than I mean it but she's got me so fucking flustered I don't even know how to talk to her anymore. If I don't bark at her, I'm likely to just kiss her, and right now she's acting odd and I need to get Birch and his girl out of my hair so I can find out what's up.

"What set Cami off just now?" Birch asks as I hand over the keys.

His tone insinuates that it's my fault that Cami's pacing the parking lot with her phone in her hand. I can see her through the dining room windows. It looks like she's in tears and I don't want to get into with my brother right now.

When I deflect with a joke, Maggie speaks up in Cami's defense and damn if it doesn't make me feel good knowing she's got my girl's back-- even if they think I don't.

Birch and Maggie are finally out my hair and I can go after my girl.

Chapter Four

Chamomile

That's it. I've had enough. I've had enough of Moonshine Ridge and enough of Cedar McAllister and enough of that drunk asshole that can't take a hint.

And all stupid Cedar has to say to me is that he "still needs to talk" after closing and tells me not to go anywhere.

I don't want to cause a scene in front of his brother and Birch's new friend, so I'm waiting in the parking lot till they leave. Trying to find out if there's any way to get off this damn mountain before next Tuesday since the shuttle came this morning and it only runs on Tuesdays.

"Cam, get back in here."

Cedar's mad. Like really mad, not his usual grumpy bosshole self.

If he thinks he's firing me over this, he's got another

think coming though. I already told him I'm out of here, I meant it.

Putting my escape plan on hold, I shove my phone in the back pocket of my jean skirt and stomp inside while Cedar holds the door open.

Inside, the bartender, Ben is standing in the hallway that leads back to the bar with a worried look on his face and I can hear a lot of raised voices from the bar.

"Wait right here," Cedar orders as he steers me into his office. Then he heads back out and down the hall.

I can hear him talking to Ben and I can hear the guys in the bar shouting and I don't know what Bennie's version of the story is but there's no way I'm going to sit in here and let that asshole Hayle and his buddies talk to Cedar without me there to defend myself.

Just as I'm about to head into the hallway from Cedar's office, he's pushing me back inside. His broad chest is a wall of muscle blocking my path and there's no getting around him as he crowds me into the small room and slams the door behind him.

"Let me see," he demands, his hands reaching for me before I have a chance to step aside.

"What are you doing?"

"Let. Me. See. Cami." Cedar has his hand wrapped around my wrist and he's turning me so my arm is in the light.

His fingers are gentle as he lifts the sleeve of my t-shirt up to my shoulder and when I turn to look at him, his face is beet red. Those full lips I've thought about having on my body so many times pressed together in a firm line.

My eyes travel down my own arm to where he's running a finger over my skin, causing goose bumps to prick up all over my body.

Dark marks have already formed where Hayle had his hand. The unmistakable imprint of his fingers showing in purples and greens around my arm.

"Where else did he touch you?"

"What?"

"Ben said he had his hands on you. Where? Show me, Chamomile. Where did the bastard touch you?"

"M-my thigh, here."

I've never seen Cedar mad before. I've never seen *anyone* as mad as Cedar is right now.

My skirt is one of those cutoff denim numbers, it covers plenty but it stops well above my knees. Right now I reach down and lift the frayed edge, pulling it gingerly up my thigh and Cedar's not the only one who inhales sharply at the sight of the angry bruise peeking around the edge from the back of my thigh.

"Anywhere else?"

Cedar's voice is low. Really low. Dangerous low in a way that has the hair on the back of my neck standing up and every nerve in my body on alert.

He runs his hand along the bruise on my thigh and I swear I swoon at his touch. It's just a little whimper that comes out and I mostly manage to hold it in.

"Does that hurt?"

The anger is still simmering there, but now there's something else in Cedar's eyes. His hand rests gently against my thigh.

I shake my head.

"It's OK," I whisper, silently willing him to move his hand higher.

There's a flash of something in his eyes when he looks up at me and then he's gone. Turning on his heel, throwing open the office door and stomping down the hall to the bar, his foot steps so heavy it shakes the floorboards.

I hear the door that separates the main restaurant and kitchen from the bar swing so hard it sounds like it breaks off its hinges and Cedar yelling so loud it really does shake the rafters.

Cedar

He fucking touched her.

I'm going to kill that sonofabitch.

Someone should have put Hayle Hart out of his misery years ago, to be honest. He's always been an asshole but I swear he gets worse with age.

I've put up with him and his buddies causing shit in the bar, because everyone in town knows he's a sorry SOB. He drinks too much, he talks shit, he leaves his tab open and I have to track him down and come after the money, but this time he's gone too far.

If he'd put his hands on *any* of my staff, I'd have him hauled out of here by the sheriff, but Cami? Touching *my* girl is going to earn him more than a night in the drunk tank. He'll be lucky if he gets out of here without an ambulance.

The bar door swings open so hard I can hear the wall behind it give way but I don't give a fuck, I'll patch it later.

"Cedar! I swear man, we were just joking around, ya know." Rapid Jones is stupid enough to get between me and Hayle.

Rapid's a big guy but I've got two inches, forty pounds, and a whole lot of pissed off over him right now. When he tries to hold me back by putting his hands on my chest, I shove past him easily.

Based on how fast he gets the fuck out of my way when he sees the look on my face, I guess he's not that stupid after all.

Somewhere off to the side, I register Ozzie Lancaster holding on to a pool cue.

I don't think any of Hayle's drinking buddies are dumb enough to try to get involved in this but if Oz thinks he's breaking my own pool cue over my head he's going down with his friend.

Sure enough, by the time I catch Hayle and haul the drunk asshole to his feet by the front of his shirt, Oz has put the cue back on the rack and moved over next to Rapid.

"Oh hey, buddy," Hayle says, his breath reeking of the cheapest whiskey we have in the bar, "I was just sayin' your new waitress is a cute one, wasn't I, guys?"

Over my shoulder I hear shuffling from his buddies that tells me they want nothing to do with this.

"I've told you to watch yourself in here before, Hart," I seethe between gritted teeth.

Even three sheets to the wind, Hayle's a strong motherfucker. He manages to break free of my grip and takes a wobbly step backwards.

"Errm whaddaya gunna do, McAllister?" He slurs.

My fist answers that question with a loud crack of cartilage as my knuckles make contact with his nose.

Hayle doesn't go down with the first punch, but his head snaps backward hard and blood spray paints the concrete floor of the bar.

It's possible that it's the booze, but I've known Hayle since he was nothing but a school yard bully giving me and brothers shit when we were growing up; my bet is that Hayle Hart wouldn't have enough sense to walk away right now if he was dead cold sober.

He lunges toward me, his left hand balled into a fist, but if he thinks I've forgotten he's a south paw, he's dumber than he is drunk.

Another hit and he's down. This time he feels that busted nose. His hand is covering his face, blood pouring onto the floor.

"Cami's mine." I'm not mincing words as I put a boot against his chest. "You're out of here for good this time, Hart, and if you ever touch my woman again there will not be enough of you left to identify, you got it?"

Hayle garbles something through the blood and the pain that sounds like he's done fighting back so I give him a shove with my boot and turn to his friends.

Rapid and Oz are standing by the bar and Bennie's staring in shock at the big man bleeding on the floor.

"Get him out of my bar," I tell the guys, "get him off my property and make sure he remembers our conversation when he sobers up because I don't mind telling him again."

The guys rush over and grab Hayle by the arm pits, dragging him out of the bar on his ass.

They've got a two hour drive down the grade if they're going to take him to the emergency room in Slow Valley and God knows they're going to have to call someone who hasn't been drinking to do the driving.

Mostly likely they'll wake Doc Everett up and have her patch him up in her office here on the ridge.

Waving a hand toward Ben to indicate that cleaning up that mess is not his job, I spin on my heel.

I need to get back to Chamomile. Need to make sure she's OK and tell her-- *everything*. How I can't stop thinking about her. That I can't live another night without making her mine for real. That--

Cami's face peeks around the edge of the broken door from the hallway that leads down to the kitchen.

She obviously saw the whole thing, but I can't tell what she's thinking now. As I come toward her, her eyes are wide as saucers, her fair skin flushed and those full breasts of hers rising and falling rapidly with her short, quick breaths.

"Cam--"

Shit. Did I just fuck everything up?

Chapter Five

Chamomile

It's wrong that I'm so turned on right now, right? I mean, watching a man punch another guy out for touching me isn't supposed to make my panties this wet, is it?

Violence isn't hot.

Except in this situation it definitely is.

Cedar just dropped a dude that's at least as big as he is.

For me.

And then he told Hayle that I'm *his woman*.

He said it like he was staking a claim, daring the men in the bar room to challenge him. Which turns out to also be hot.

But did he mean it?

I stand huddled against the doorway, where the bar door is, indeed, hanging on by one hinge and the frame is cracked and splintered where the other hinge was ripped out of the wood.

When the guys have managed to pull their bleeding buddy out of the bar and Cedar motions at Ben like he's saying he'll take care of the clean up later, I poke my head a little further around the edge of the doorway.

I'm breathing so hard right now I can't catch my breath and if Cedar tells me to, I would totally bend over one of the bar tables right here right now and let him do anything he wants to.

Anything.

But when Cedar sees me peering from around the corner, that intensely possessive look vanishes from his face.

"Cam--"

His voice just goes dead. He obviously didn't mean for me to see what just happened.

As Cedar comes closer, I move backward. Away from the bar and anyone left in it. Cedar follows me as I lead him back to his office, but now his gorgeous face is lined in regrets that I can't bear to think he's having.

Was what happened with Hayle back there just a heat of the moment thing? Was it just Cedar being protective of one of his staff members? Was he even thinking about the words he was spitting in Hayle's face?

I stop moving when my ass hits the edge of his desk. Then I stand there, my hands holding to the edges of the desk beside my thighs trying to look calm when in reality, I need to hang on to something solid to keep from shaking.

Cedar closes the office door behind him, his bulk blocking the only exit from the small, windowless room where he does his inventory and payroll.

"Cam." He sounds more like himself again. With that rough voice and a hint of grumpiness at the edges. "Sorry, I didn't mean for you to watch that. Hayle's always been trouble but I've never known him to put his hands on a woman. If I'd known he was that kind of problem I'd have eighty-sixed him long ago."

Cedar's eyes are pinned on the hem of my skirt where he saw the bruises before.

"Did you mean it?" It's the only thing on my mind. I have to know.

His head tilts so slightly to the side. "Fuck yeah, Cam, I'd never let anyone in here that thinks they can treat my staff like that. I--"

"No, Cedar, I mean..."

Letting go of my grip on the desk is risky. I can feel my heart pounding and my knees are jelly, but I push away from the safety of the solid surface and take one tentative step forward. It's all the space I can move before I'd be literally touching him chest to chest and I don't think I can handle that quite yet.

"Did you mean what you told him? What you told all of them? When you said I was *yours?*"

Cedar and I are so close now that I can feel the heat

from his body. I swear I can hear his heart beating; fast and hard and loud, or maybe that's mine.

He stares down at me and I refuse to look away. I watch a storm rage through his eyes before he finally says anything.

"I wanted you to stay after closing tonight so I could talk to you about something important."

Cedar

Am I supposed to hold her? Pull her into my arms? Sit down and pull her into my lap? What are the rules for this?

My hands start to reach up to wrap around her upper arms and then I remember she has bruises there too and anger rises up in me all over again.

And dammit if Cami isn't just standing there!

Those perfect tits of hers an inch away from brushing my chest. There's no space behind me so I can't step back, I can't get around her, there's no damn room to breathe in this office, and those sea green eyes are hers are locked on mine while she waits for an answer that I'm afraid is going to be wrong.

Because yeah, I fucking meant it. Cami's mine, all right. But for some reason, I feel like I can tell anyone but her.

What if she doesn't feel the same way?

"OK fine then."

Cami's words are barely intelligible, muttered low under her breath. Her gaze falls and so do her shoulders as she takes a step sideways as if she's going for the door behind me.

"Yes."

The heel of my boot kicks back against the bottom of the office door and there's not a chance in hell I'm going to let her out of here.

My arms catch her up and take her backwards, lifting her easily onto the desk. I wedge myself between her knees, causing the rough hem of her denim skirt to ride up high on her thighs to make room for me.

A glimpse of cotton panties peeks into view, threatening to distract me before I press my hands to each side of her face and force her to look back up at me.

"You're mine, Chamomile," I growl only inches from her face. "You were mine the moment I saw you and every day that I haven't been able to claim you has been pure fucking hell, OK?"

"Maybe you don't feel the same way about me, but I'll be damned if I'll let another man think he can touch you. Do you hear me?"

Her pink lips are swollen to a dark rose and parted as if she's begging for me to kiss her just as roughly as I want to.

I might be a weak man, but I'm not an asshole that's going to take what I want without permission, so when she doesn't say anything, I relax the pressure I have against her face and I swear letting go of her is the hardest thing I've ever willed my muscles to do.

"Are you kidding me right now, Cedar?"

Cami's small hand grabs the front of my shirt and the material twists violently in her fist as she pulls me back to her.

"You can't just not kiss me after all that," she scolds before pulling me to her, firmly, fully, until my entire world consists of nothing but her lips on mine.

Chapter Six

Chamomile

Cedar's lips seal to mine. His tongue teases inside my mouth and I open for him, letting him teach my tongue how to dance with his.

His hands are against my face again, his fingers wrapping around the back of my head and threading into my hair and undoing my braid.

When he moves closer I moan into our kiss.

My thighs part wider to make room for him but he's too tall for the height of the desk. I can't fit against him the way my body is aching to.

Like he knows what I need, he reaches between us and presses his fingers between my legs. The pressure is everything I'm craving and this time the noise I make is more than a moan.

"Fuck baby, you're wet." His voice is coarse sandpaper against my ear. "Tell me this sweet little pussy is wet because of me."

His finger slips under the edge of my panties and drags through my slit. It feels so good that I'm lifting my ass off the edge of the desk, desperate to get closer to him.

"It's because of you, Cedar," I promise as I drop my head back and rock against his hand. "I've never been this wet before and it's all because of you."

There's a deep chuckle against my skin where he's nipping lightly at my neck. "Never, baby?"

The finger that's been teasing me slides inside me in a firm stroke and it's such a new feeling I can't catch my breath. There's a pressure building that I've never felt before.

"Cedar," I pant, "is this what an orgasm feels like?"

If it is, sign me up for more. It's not the *"falling apart"* feeling I read about but having his finger stroking in and out of me is definitely building up to something.

Until he stops and gives me a weird look that makes me realize I just said something really stupid.

"You've never had an orgasm before, baby?" He sounds incredulous.

I guess I understand why.

When I shake my head no, he steps from between my thighs, taking that magic hand with him and leaving me feeling needy and disappointed.

"At all? Or just with a man?"

Oh boy. Here we go. I should have kept my mouth shut. It figures that a man like Cedar would prefer a woman that knows what she's doing. Someone who's been past second base.

"Never. I've never been with a man."

The look on Cedar's face has me pulling the hem of my skirt down and looking for my purse. So much for being his woman, I guess.

"Whoa." Cedar's hands grip my knees and hold me in place. "Where do you think you're going?"

"You stopped," I point out. "I get it, you know, if you aren't into-- *teaching*. Most guys want women who already know what to do. I don't blame you for changing your mind."

The sound Cedar makes is so feral it should scare me but it doesn't. It rumbles all the way through me and causes a new surge of wetness to soak my panties, that tug in my belly flaring up needy and urgent.

"This is mine, Chamomile." His hand snakes between my thighs and cups my pussy. "You're mine. I'm yours. And you are not going surrender that sweet cherry to me on my fucking desk here at work, you understand?"

Nodding in a trance, I let him take my hand and pull me back to my feet.

"We're still doing this though, right?" I ask as he hands my bag to me and grabs the keys to his truck.

"Damn straight we are," he mutters, taking my hand and tugging me through the closed restaurant and out the front doors, barely bothering to turn off the lights and lock the doors behind us before buckling me into his truck and driving me to his house.

Cedar

A better man would call a time out. Would, I don't know, drop her off at her place. Kiss her goodnight. Take a step-- or two or ten-- back and take her out on a real date. Buy her some damn flowers and make sure she understands that this isn't just about getting in those wet little white cotton panties that I'm dying to bury my nose in.

Maybe that's how it would have happened if tonight had gone like I'd planned. If we'd had a mature conversation after work like I'd intended. If I'd been able to confess my feelings for her without breaking someone's nose.

I don't know. Maybe we'd have dated for a few weeks before I dragged her into my bed, but there's no turning back now. Especially when Cami's curves are pressed against me in the middle of the bench seat of my truck and her hand is resting impossibly high on my thigh while her finger traces tiny designs on the denim of my jeans.

My dick strains behind my fly like it's reaching toward her touch that's agonizingly out of reach.

This might be the first time I've regretted building

the house so far from the tavern. It's really only about three miles, out on the edges of what we consider town in these parts. At the time, I wanted to put some distance between me and work but now it's the longest damn three miles of my life.

Cam's hand moves almost imperceptibly closer to my inner thigh and I can feel the hint her hand resting against my swollen balls.

I reach down and move her hand so that it's right on top of me.

"Baby, that's all yours, you can touch me anytime you want."

My hand covers hers, making sure she can feel the ridge of my cock. I want her to know what she does to me.

Her fingers flex and tease, finding their way around my girth and giving me a squeeze.

"Fuck baby," I grind out between my teeth, "you feel that, don't you? Feel what you do to me? You've have me like this for weeks."

"Exaggerate much?" She sasses with another squeeze before running her hand up my length.

The sexiest fucking gasp comes out of her lips when her fingers find the tip of my dick poking out of the waistband of my jeans already oozing precum.

"Doesn't that hurt?" She asks, running her finger across the wet tip and looking up at me when I flinch under her delicate touch.

"Not when you do that," I rasp out, desperately

throwing the truck in park as soon as I pull up in front of the front deck of my house.

"You like teasing me?"

I see the wicked smile on her face when she pushes her hand under my belt and into my jeans, wiggling her slender fingers around the crown of my dick, making the whole unit surge with need.

"It's only teasing if I don't put out, right?"

That wicked smile grows as she looks up at me.

So my girl likes being naughty, does she? I shouldn't be surprised.

"Get in my bed before I fuck you here in the truck."

I can see it too, pulling Cami's thick thigh over my crotch till she's straddling me while I ruck up that little skirt till it's around her waist and pull her panties aside so she can slide down on my cock.

That's definitely happening. Not tonight though.

My girl's first time isn't going to be awkwardly tangled around the steering wheel of a pick-up like we were teenagers rutting in an orchard down in Keller's Ferry after homecoming.

Tonight, I'm going to show her what it's like to be with a man.

Chapter Seven

Chamomile

Inside, Cedar promises me he'll show me the house later and I'm glad that he's not suddenly wanting to play host.

All I want is to get him naked so I can touch him some more. I love the way he reacts when I touch him and I'm eager to see what he'll do when I put him in my mouth.

Cedar stops me before we head down a hallway, catching my face in his hands again and leaning down for another one of those kisses that makes my toes curl.

I have to grab onto the front of his shirt to keep my balance when his lips leave mine.

"Do you need anything, baby?" he whispers so sweetly before we move.

"You," I tell him. "I need you."

There's more than hunger in Cedar's dark eyes.

When he looks at me I see promises that go well beyond tonight and I know my life is about to change forever.

It doesn't scare me at all though. I want this. Not just making love to Cedar, but everything with Cedar.

His bedroom is at the end of a wide hallway through double doors and a huge bed is centered between two night stands on the wall directly in front of the doors.

"Lights on or off, baby?"

His hand rests against my back between my shoulder blades and I lean back into his touch.

"On," I answer, "I want to see you."

Cedar's nostrils flare as he inhales sharply like he just touched a live wire. The over head lights flick on but they're on a dimmer because they lower from the harsh bright white to a softer glow that's still plenty to see by.

"Get on the bed," Cedar commands, moving me in that direction.

I kick off my boots and crawl up on his bed on all fours.

"Fucking tease," he laughs darkly, and then his hand comes down on my ass cheek with a slap that spreads a tingle all the way through me.

Then my skirt is up around my waist, Cedar's large hands grab me by my hips and pull me to the edge of the bed so that I'm barely propped up on my knees.

He buries his face between my legs from behind and I feel his breath hot and damp against the spot in my panties that are already soaked through.

"Fuuuuuck. Chamomile," he groans against me, "you're heaven, baby, you know that, right?"

With a tap to my hip I flip over for him, and watch with wide eyes as he pulls his t-shirt over his head.

My mouth goes dry at the sight of him. Flat pecs and carved abs covered in a light dusting of dark hair with a thicker trail down the center of his chest that disappears below the waist of his jeans.

So that's why they call it a happy trail.

I want to touch all of him. I want to kiss him and run my tongue over every muscle. My hands reach up and run over his skin. His eyes close and he breathes heavy. My fingers are at work on his belt buckle when he reaches down and pulls my shirt over my head.

Then I'm on my back, moving into the center of the bed to make room for Cedar as he crawls up between my knees.

In seconds I'm naked, my thighs spread wide with Cedar between them, and if I thought he made me feel good back in his office, this is more than I thought was possible.

His mouth is so hot on my sex and his tongue drags through my slit like I'm his favorite flavor of ice cream.

I'm so wet for him I can hear the sound when he pushes a finger inside me like he did before. He works it in and slides it back out a few times while he continues to lick through my pussy.

"You want to know what it feels like to get off baby?"

His voice is thick and raspy, talking dirty to me between kisses along the hinge of my thigh.

I nod, writhing against his hand, begging him to move his finger inside me again.

"Because I'm going to make you come for me, Cam."

He gives me what I'm begging for, his finger strokes me from inside and then he pushes a second finger in deep with the first. I'm seeing stars. I feel an impossible pressure building up in my core. I'm not sure what's coming next, I don't know what to expect, but I know I need it. Whatever Cedar is doing to me, I need him to carry it through to the end.

"You are gorgeous, Chamomile. I love that I'm the only one who's ever seen you like this, that I'm the only one who's ever going to see you like this. I need to you let go and surrender to me now. I want you to come for me like a good girl."

I feel his mouth on my sex again but now his tongue is concentrating on that spot that makes me jump. His fingers sliding in and out of me faster, wetter, stroking me from inside while his mouth suctions down against my clit.

Holy shit. I am not prepared for this. The feeling is so intense, I don't know if I want to chase after it or run away from it but Cedar doesn't give me the option to escape it.

Soon I'm moving with the sensations, bucking wildly and riding Cedar's face and hand, vaguely aware that I have my hand tangled in that dark hair of his as I completely break into pieces like a dream.

Cedar

As soon as Cami's cream is coating my beard I know I'll never get enough of making this sweet girl come. She tastes like paradise and the sounds she makes while she wiggles against my touch, her soft body aching for that release? My fantasies have nothing on the real thing.

When she bucks and screams my name right before giving in and letting the orgasm take hold of her, I feel like so damn proud for giving that to her.

Knowing that I'm the only man who will ever see her come undone like that has my cock so hard it's pulsing with a primal need to sink into her wet heat and claim her for real.

I kiss her tenderly, stroking her gently and letting her body recuperate as much as I can manage but I'm not a patient man tonight.

"Need you now, baby," I moan against her soft belly as I kiss my way back up her body. "You think you're ready to take me inside you, Cam?"

When I kiss her I know she can taste her juices on my mouth and in my beard and it drives me to thrust my hardness against her mound when she sucks my tongue greedily instead of being turned off.

"I'm ready, Cedar," she tells me.

Her hand reaches down and wraps around the base of my shaft and fuck! I want her hands all over me. I know this isn't the slow exploration of each other's bodies that she deserves but I've already been in agony for so long.

I need her.

She steers me toward her opening and holds me as I push the head of my dick just barely past her gate.

"I'm not wearing anything, Cam." It's not a observation, it's a declaration. I mean it, I want this woman all over me, her scent, her juices. I need to feel the texture of her channel as she takes me into her body and squeezes me while I stretch her to fit me.

"You understand what I'm saying?" My eyes lock with her pretty green ones and I move forward just a tiny bit more with her hand still gripping the root of my cock.

Cami nods slowly.

"I don't want you to, Cedar," she says breathlessly, "I want to feel you, just you."

She moves her hand and there's nothing left to stop me.

I push in, taking it as slow as I'm able to, knowing the extra tightness strangling my cock is going to give way any second and I don't want this to hurt for Cam.

"Wait." She whimpers beneath me, her fingers clenching my shoulder with her nails digging in.

Sweat beads on my brow as I force myself to stay still for her.

Cami takes a few deep breaths and relaxes her thighs, letting them fall open farther for me and then she's rocking up toward me.

"Go," she begs. "Please Cedar, fuck me."

In one smooth motion I slide all the way in. Letting Cami's tight sheath grip me as I fill her body.

When I bottom out balls deep in her heat I don't have any control left. I'm running on pure primal instinct to claim her entirely.

I draw back and the little disappointed noise she makes at the loss of my cock filling her tight pussy has me slamming back into her with a feral hunger. Again and again, with Cami's fingers gripping me by the back of my neck and then by my hips.

She keeps saying my name and begging for more and then I feel her walls start to flutter around my shaft. I hear her breathing change and as I watch those green eyes go cloudy and unfocused while her sweet tunnel clamps down on me, I'm going with her.

My balls tighten and I'm pumping rope after rope of my sticky seed into her womb. Coating her insides and marking her as mine forever.

We lie together for a long time, catching our breath. I pepper her face with soft, grateful kisses till my softening member reluctantly slides from her body.

"Wait here." I kiss her lightly and my heart clenches at the sight of her sleepy, satisfied face as I head for the bathroom.

"Let me know if this stings," I tell her when I return with a warm wet wash cloth.

Chamomile opens her pretty thighs for me and let's me clean her. Her sex is swollen and red from rough love making and the wash clothes comes away with a hint of pink from the remnants of her virginity.

Again, I swell with pride and gratitude that she chose me to be her first.

Her only.

Epilogue 1

Epilogue 1

Six Months Later

Chamomile

Now that Birch and Maggie's wedding is over with, it's mine and Cedar's turn.

We'll be doing a quick thing on Nan's property a couple of weeks from now, right before Thanksgiving when my parents can be here for both the wedding and the holiday and get to know the McAllister clan their baby girl is joining.

It's supposed to be just friends and family but when you marry the guy who owns the only local tavern and hotel in a town as small as Moonshine Ridge? Well, let's just say that Nan is prepared to feed everyone on the mountain.

Our own baby plans haven't interfered with our

wedding plans so far and even though I'm so jealous of Ash and Hyacinth's baby, Rose, and now Birch and Maggie just announced they're expecting in spring; I'm also grateful for the time that Cedar and I get to be just the two of us.

I have to admit that I'll miss chasing him through the house naked when we have to worry about little ones catching us in the act.

In the meantime, I get my baby fix by watching Rose so Ash and Hy can still get their adult time too.

For a girl who stepped off a shuttle bus in a town she'd never been to where she didn't know a soul, my life has become so full in just six months.

Suddenly I have a huge family-- so different from my own experience as an only child-- with three protective brothers with hearts of gold, two new sisters who quickly became my best friends as well and we're all pretty sure Violet will be joining the family officially soon too, so make that three BFF sisters!

Nieces and nephews are beginning to arrive and here at home? I have my own, personal mountain man who might not be my boss anymore, but he still likes to boss me around-- in all the best ways.

And in just a couple more weeks, Cedar will become my husband.

Then we'll start getting serious about filling these mountains with another branch of the McAllister family tree.

Epilogue 2

Epilogue 2
Five Years Later
Cedar

Fall on the ridge is always hit or miss. The year Cam and I got hitched, it was seventy degrees and sunny in Nan's back forty on November twenty-two.

I'll never forget that day, the day Chamomile stood up in front of God and everyone we know to become my wife.

Five years later and there's already a foot of snow covering the ground outside a week before our fifth anniversary.

"Hey baby, you want anything while I'm up?" I bend down and kiss my wife's cheek on my way to grab another pitcher of the house's signature dark beer here at the Brick and Porter.

"Another ginger-ale would be nice."

I take Cami's glass from her and head for the bar of the pizza joint.

When Current Jones and his wife opened the brick oven pizza place with the small batch brewery in house a couple years back, I wasn't sure what to think. For starters, I'd gotten used to being the only game in town when it came to both food and drinks and I wasn't sure if I wanted the competition. Plus, Moonshine Ridge had been ticking along just fine without any of the craft beer snobbery that's taken over down in Slow River.

I gotta admit, it's damn nice to have some place to enjoy a beer and something to eat without having to go into my own damn work to get it.

"'Nother pitcher?" Ginger Jones asks as she takes the empty pitcher that I just set down on the bar between us.

"And ginger ale for my girl," I tell her, handing her Cam's empty.

"She still not feeling good with this one?" Ginger asks, placing her hand below her own swollen belly as she holds the new pitcher under the tap.

"Not like the others," I admit, looking back at my wife with her feet propped up on the river rock hearth of the big stone fireplace where we're enjoying our afternoon with Cypress and Violet.

It took us over a year to get pregnant but once we did, it seems like Cami's been knocked up for three years straight. She loved being pregnant with the girls, but this one's been different. She tires easily and the nausea hangs around most of the day.

"Betcha this one's a boy," Ginger predicts, setting the new pitcher on the counter and grabbing filing a fresh glass of ginger-ale for Cam. "When do you find out?"

"Next month." I sigh, dropping another couple bucks in Ginger's tip jar before grabbing up the drinks.

"If it's a boy, I'll comp your next pie." Ginger gives me a wink and makes her way back to the kitchen. I'm pretty sure she'll be off for maternity leave herself by the time we have the answer.

When I come back to where we've taken over the selection of seating by the big stone fireplace, I take a look at my newest sister-in-law tucked under Cypress's arm like a baby bird.

"How about you, Vi? Do you need anything?" I ask.

My eldest brother growls at me as I fill his pint glass.

"I'm already up, Cypress," I tell him.

"Do you need anything baby?" Cypress turns and asks his wife, "It's no trouble, you want me to go down to the bakery and get you some of them croissants you like?"

Cami's hand reaches up and she curls her fingers around mine. I hand her soda to her and smile when her eyes meet mine.

"Baby, I'm good, really, just sit and enjoy your time with your brothers." Violet scolds Cypress with a swat to his arm.

"Mountain men, amirite?" Vi jokes, rolling her eyes and making Cami giggle.

Cypress moves in closer to his wife on the double seat they're sharing by the fire. His arm moving protectively around her shoulder.

Violet and Cypress are only on baby number one. They had a hard time getting their family started and they came down from the cabin for Vi's doctor appointment this afternoon. Cypress has never been good around people but he'd do anything for his wife and that includes sitting in the pizza place on a snowy November day having a beer with his brothers while she enjoys being pregnant at the same time as her sister in law. But prying Cypress's arm off his wife isn't an option.

The family reunion is in full swing, with Ash and Hyacinth stopping by after they close up the sporting goods shop for the day and then Birch and Maggie stop by for a bit just to not get left out.

The snow outside is blowing pretty hard and I feel good knowing that Cypress and Violet have already planned to stay in one of the cottages at the lodge instead of heading back up the mountain tonight.

We're laughing it up and talking about Thanksgiving dinner plans this year up at our folks house-- Nan's still as ornery as old ladies get, but she's slowing down enough that Mom and Dad have taken over the big family gatherings.

The bell over the front door dings as it opens and a burst of frozen air and a few snow flurries blow in around the man wearing a pea coat and wool beanie as he pushes through the door.

I almost don't recognize him.

He's lost the gut and bulked up the muscle. His beard is grown out full and red and his nose bears the the unmistakable shape of someone who's been punched good and hard a couple of times.

"Hey Cedar," Hayle says quietly with a chin nod toward me. "Chamomile." He says much more softly with a respectful nod toward my wife.

The room is silent and all eyes are on me.

Hayle Hart hasn't been seen around the Ridge since I broke the fucker's nose five years ago.

"Hart." I say by way of greeting.

"Hi Hayle." My wife gives him a smile he doesn't deserve but she tucks herself closer under my arm and I like the way she makes it clear who she belongs to.

Hayle gives a silent nod to the rest of my clan and keeps on walking all the way to the back room of the joint. Putting plenty of space between us.

"So that was-- civil?" Maggie says, the question clear in her voice.

"Yeah," Cam answers. "He came by to talk when he got back in town a few days ago. We're OK."

"The day Hayle Hart is 'OK' is the day I shave my beard," Birch grumbles.

Let's hope it doesn't come to that.

Next in the McAllister Men of Moonshine Ridge
Cypress

I'm happy for my brothers, really, but I'm not cut out for that kind of life: Living in town, running a business, settling down with a woman and filling her up with my babies.

I'm content up here in my cabin, living off the grid and keeping busy with my animals.

Until I meet a woman who really gets my goat. Literally.

Violet's a vision in a sundress and sandals when she finds me out in the field to ask if Alfred belongs to me.

I want to tell her that old goat isn't the only one that belongs to me, but any fool can see that a woman like Violet isn't going to let a rough old grump like me steal her away to the mountains and claim her as his own.

Until she shares her secret with me and I know I can't let her go.

Finding the Mountain Man

The McAllister Men of Moonshine Ridge

About

Cypress McAllister

I'm happy for my brothers, really, but I'm not cut out for that kind of life: Living in town, running a business, settling down with a woman and filling her up with my babies.

I'm content up here in my cabin, living off the grid and keeping busy with my animals.

Until I meet a woman who really gets my goat. Literally.

Violet's a vision in a sundress and sandals when she finds me out in the field to ask if Alfred belongs to me.

I want to tell her that old goat isn't the only one that belongs to me, but any fool can see that a woman like Violet isn't going to let a rough old grump like me steal her away to the mountains and claim her as his own.

Until she shares her secret with me and I know this is where she belongs: with me, on my mountain, growing our children inside her.

Cypress and Violet

Finding the Mountain Man

The McAllister Men of Moonshine Ridge
by
Rocklyn Ryder

Chapter One

Violet

"OK then, I guess we'll see you next weekend."

My cousin, Maggie, throws her arms around my neck and squeezes tight as I promise to come back up to Moonshine Ridge at the end of the week for the wedding rehearsal and dinner afterward.

Birch gives me a quick squeeze as well and before I can head out, I have to make my way through the entire McAllister family with hugs and handshakes, laughing at inside jokes and an extra special goodbye to baby Rose even though the eight week old baby obliviously sleeps through my cooing and kisses in her mother's arms.

Finally, I climb into my car and head back to Keller's Ferry where I've been staying.

Maggie and Birch are getting married next weekend, and I'm the maid of honor.

It's been a whirlwind of a summer for me; discovering a new connection to a long lost side of my family tree and pretty much hitting it off with Magnolia from our first conversation. And I was so happy that I was able to fill in some gaps and straighten out the record in Birch's own family history in the process.

Thank heavens for great aunt Clara's diary. Oops...I mean Eliza, I guess. Anyway, the whole McAllister family was excited to learn the truth about the controversial mystery their ancestor had been caught up in and I gained an entire adoptive family in the process.

That's how I ended up being included in the family photo shoot this morning up at Serenity Springs.

The rest of the clan is staying at the resort for the rest of the week; camped out in fancy wall tents with real furniture, relaxing in the hot springs and wreaking general havoc on the camping resort that their friends, the Diaz family, run up at the end of the road.

I have to leave early, this section of the highway is barely even two lanes in some places and it'll take me awhile just to get back down to Moonshine Ridge-- where most of the McAllisters live-- and another hour or so to get down to Keller's Ferry so I can follow up on the phone calls I need to make.

Another ten miles of twisting mountain road left till I reach town. "Town" being Moonshine Ridge, where I'll be able to stop and grab a pop from Nan's general store, where Pepper is working today while Nan is up at the resort with the family, before heading the rest of the way down the mountain.

Finding the Mountain Man

I would love to just move up here and settle in for the long haul. If only that was an option.

Moonshine Ridge is crawling with hot, bearded mountain men and I've never been anywhere I felt like I was home like I do in the small mountain town, but the ridge is sorely lacking in job opportunities.

It's about here that the dread starts creeping in. Right now, I'm surrounded by tall pine trees and the smell of the forest duff and rich soil, incense cedars, and fresh mountain air. This is my happy place and the closer I get to civilization, the more the old anxieties start to buzz in my head.

Which is probably why I don't see the goat right away.

It steps off the shoulder of the road and walks directly in front of my car as I come around a curve, and then stares at me, nonchalantly chewing its cud as I come to a hasty stop just a few feet from hitting it.

When I hit the horn, he doesn't flinch.

"Goat! Go! Go, goat, go!" I yell from the open window, not entirely unaware that I sound like I'm reading a kindergarten book.

Goat does not go.

This must be why the saying is "stubborn as a goat."

Maybe I could just drive around him, but he's got a collar on with a bell and he's so cute with his floppy brown ears. This stretch of road gets a lot more traffic than you'd think and I can't stand the thought of this guy becoming road kill. Besides, the collar makes me think maybe somebody would miss him.

Pulling off to the side of the road, I roll up the windows and kill the engine.

"OK, buddy, let's get you back home," I tell-- Alfred. His name is imprinted into the leather of his collar and it's easy to read when I grab hold and pull him off the road.

"Is this where you live?"

If the narrow dirt road leading up the hill from the side of the road goes to Alfred's home address, the goat is not telling.

From here I can't see where the dirt track leads.

"Is that your driveway, Alfred?" I ask the goat.

Alfred makes a distinctly goat-like noise and nudges me with his nose. Which is kinda sweet and also kinda gross because I'm wearing a short sundress and Alfred isn't exactly clean.

No way I'm putting him in my car.

"Looks like we're going for a walk, buddy." I tug on his collar and he walks along easily with me as we round the first bend of the narrow lane.

Definitely someone's driveway, I conclude as soon as the first "private property" sign comes into view.

Definitely someone who does not want company. As Alfred and I make our way past more "no trespassing," and "dead end, no turn around," signs I start wondering if maybe I should just leave Alfred here to fend for himself.

Finding the Mountain Man

The driveway is long and it winds up a steep hill from the main road, curving around the natural lay of the land in a big loop so that when I first see the small farm come into view I'm stunned.

I don't know what I was expecting but it wasn't the cleared acreage with the long cabin overlooking an expansive meadow with the steep granite mountain looming protectively behind it.

A final sign at the end of driveway reads, "Warning, Attack goat on duty."

"Is that supposed to be you?" I narrow my eyes and give Alfred a dubious glare.

Alfred head butts me gently in the hip.

I spot movement out in a fenced field on the other side of the cabin and tug Alfred in that direction.

"Let's go tell them their attack goat was trying to hitch a ride out of here," I tell him as we head toward the field where I saw someone moving about a minute ago.

Cypress

Sinking the blade of the shovel deep into the earth I've been turned up, I head over to where I left a jug of ice water, then I strip off the t-shirt that's soaked with sweat and after drinking my fill of the cool water, I pour the rest over my head. Giving my hair a shake, I run my hand over my beard and wipe the hair off my forehead.

The shade feels good over here under the trees, but I need to get back to the field. Every year I think about how I'm not getting any younger. Every year I say I'm going to buy a tractor. Every year I'm out here with a shovel and a hoe working the land by hand.

Heading back into the field, I pull the shovel from the ground where I left it and drive it in deep again with a kick of my foot.

The animals are pretty low maintenance most of the year. The alpacas have no trouble with the uneven terrain of my property and they find plenty of grazing up on the mountain side that's not fit for farming.

The goats too, not that I ever meant to start collecting those, but when Marcia and Alex end up with too many kids for their homestead in the spring, I've been know to be an easy mark and I've taken a few off their hands over the years.

They raise their goats for meat, but I can't stand the thought of raising animals for slaughter. I know that makes me soft but I've done enough shit in this lifetime that was anything but soft, if I want to keep the alpacas for wool and goats for the hell of it, I figure I deserve some softness in my life.

When I hear a woman's voice behind me, I start thinking maybe it's time for me to get out of the sun.

"Excuse me? Sir?"

Not sure how many heat stroke fueled hallucinations would start with a woman calling me "sir." I spin around toward the sound of the voice and, fuck me, she's no hallucination. I have obviously given myself a damn heart attack out here and died and this is the angel they sent to guide me to the promised land.

On second thought-- not sure that's where I'm headed. So maybe the beautiful young lady holding Alfred by the collar is real after all.

She's a dream in a pale green dress, one of them sundresses with the skinny little straps tied in neat bows on top of her shoulders. It's got all that puckered up fabric that stretches enticingly over full breasts and a skirt that billows around her thighs in the light breeze. The whole thing is the color of the early spring sprouts and it sets off the deep bronze of her smooth skin.

Fuck me.

She's got enough curves to keep my hands full and my dick happy for a lifetime, and that smile she's giving me has my mind thinking all kinds of things that would probably send her running all the way back down to the highway if she could read my thoughts.

"Does this belong to you?" She asks, giving old Alfred a playful shove as he pulls the hem of her dress into his mouth.

I know she means Alfred, but I'm looking straight at her when I answer.

"Yes ma'am, I believe it does."

Chapter Two

Violet

When he answers, his eyes aren't on the goat, they're pinned on me with a possessive sort of hunger that has me thinking Alfred's on his own now.

This guy is out here in the sun, working hard to dig up the land with nothing but a shovel and a hoe. From the looks of those muscles, this isn't the only hard work he does up here.

He's well over six feet tall, with a full beard a shade more brown than the nearly black hair hanging in damp, loose curls where he pushes them back off his face when he wipes the sweat off his brow with the back of a thick forearm.

His brow isn't the only thing covered in sweat. He's naked to the waist, giving me an eyeful of what I'm going to be thinking about when I'm alone later.

He's all man, I swear I can smell the pheromones

from here, and he's setting the bar impossibly high for other men.

"He'll eat the whole thing if you let him," he says, giving a chin nod toward Alfred.

I only half hear what he's saying. His voice is exactly what I want to go with the picture, deep and rumbly in a way that goes through me causing my core to tighten and my panties to get damp.

"Not saying I'm going complain, ma'am." My half-naked, bearded giant breaks into a wide grin. "But you might not be as happy about it and me and Al."

Something about Alfred. The goat? Dress? What?

Snapping out of my lust-addled daze I look down at my side where Alfred has managed to pull an astonishing amount of my skirt into his mouth with his jaw working rhythmically as he munches away.

"Oh! Alfred! Stop," I scold as I tug at the fabric. "Ewww."

Goats are kinda cute to begin with and Alfred has won me over, until I manage to pull most of my dress out of his goat throat to find myself covered in goat drool.

My dress is missing a pretty sizable chunk of fabric now. Leaving my thigh exposed much higher than I'm comfortable with.

"Dang, I liked this dress," I mutter to no one in particular.

"Looks like Al likes it too."

Oh. That's right. Incredibly sex mountain man. When did he get so close?

The step I take back when he gets into my personal space is involuntary. Having him so close feels like I grabbed an electric fence, the shock is instant and nearly knocks me off my feet.

"Sorry," he gruffs, sounding embarrassed. "Didn't mean to startle you."

"It's fine. I mean, you didn't-- startle me. That's not what happened." *OK, Vi, stop trying to talk to the man, you're just making a fool of yourself,* I tell myself.

Up close like he is now, I can see that his eyes are a piercing shade of green, the kind that change color with mood. I wish knew him well enough to know what their current combination of emerald, moss, and stormy sea means but when he looks down at me there's no mistaking the way his pupils dilate and his nostrils flare.

I have a crazy impulse to touch him now that he's within reach. I want to put my hands on that broad chest and run my fingers through the hair there, tracing the patterns of the dark swirls surrounding his flat, tight nipples just to see if they're sensitive like mine.

My fingers itch. A moment of stillness passes between us and I can almost hear him telling me to do it, or maybe it's just the way his eyes darken, taking on a hint of hazel now.

I'm about to go for it when he shifts his weight and takes a step closer-- to Alfred-- totally breaking the spell.

"Sorry 'bout that." He nods toward the missing section of my dress.

Do I imagine it? Or do his nostrils flare again with a deep inhale as his eyes linger on my exposed skin longer than is really necessary?

"Let me just take care of this guy," he says, reaching to pull gently on Alfred's collar.

Cypress

Damned old goat, so stubborn when he wants to be that he might as well be a mule.

When I give his collar a tug, the bell he wears jingles but he doesn't move. Instead, he pulls back and twists his head away from me, back toward our pretty visitor. He nuzzles against her thigh where he ate away her dress and rucks the remaining fabric up high on her hip in the process.

A flash of panties the same minty green color of her dress comes into view, sending my heart rate into overdrive. I didn't think my dick could get any harder but now it surges painfully against the zipper of my old fatigues.

That glimpse of her lacy little bikinis across her copper skin and the curve of a full ass that begs to fill up my palm is going to have me beating myself raw when she's gone.

The thought of her leaving me hits me hard enough to make me unsteady on my feet. It's her I want to grab onto, haul into my arms, and keep forever, not Alfred.

"Come on, old man," I tell Al, "let's get back to the pen."

Alfred nuzzles her thigh again and she scratches his head between his horns.

"It's OK, Alfred," she coos, "we're still friends."

Squatting down to pick Al up causes the seam of my pants to cut into my aching balls and I have to adjust myself discreetly, using Alfred as a shield before I hoist the goat up in my arms and haul his ass off to the goat pen behind the barn.

He bleats in indignation as his throws his head over my should to stare back at the girl that brought him back to me, or the maybe it was Alfred that brought her to me.

"I know buddy," I whisper in the floppy brown ear that hits me in the face, "I don't want to leave her either."

"I'm just gonna toss Houdini here back in the pen," I spin around and walk backwards as I go. "Don't go anywhere."

But I guess I don't really have to worry about her taking off before I get a chance to find out who she is-- and how I can keep her-- because when I turn to talk to her she's following not far behind me.

"Ooh." The noise she makes when we round the barn has my chest clenching, I want to believe she likes my small farm up here in the mountains. I want to believe this would be enough for her, but just looking at her I can tell she's the kinda of woman that's used to all night grocery stores and dinner deliveries to her doorstep.

"Are those lamas?" She squeals, her sandals making a flopping noise against the hard-packed dirt as she runs toward the fence like an excited little kid.

"Alpacas," I correct her, dropping old Al over the top of the fence to the goat pen and knowing it take him long till he's found his way out again.

"What's the difference?"

"Not sure of all the finer points," I say, coming up close beside her. "They're related to lamas. A little smaller, mostly nicer, and their fleece makes some damn fine wool."

"They're so cute," she murmurs next to me, reaching her hand through the fence and calling to the animals, hoping to get one to come over to her.

She's so cute.

With all that thick, black hair and wild curls blowing in the mountain breeze and a smile on her face that outshines the sun.

"*Alfred!*" She scolds the old goat with a laugh, "I thought you had your own pen?"

Al's managed to find his way into the alpaca enclosure and is busy making sure he stays the center of her attention.

Never thought I'd be jealous of that damn goat, but here I am, telepathically warning him he's about to be stew if he keeps trying to steal my woman.

"I uh, probably have something you can put on," I give her just the slightest nudge of my elbow against her arm while we're still standing side by side. I don't trust myself to touch her, too afraid I'll pull her in tight and never let her go.

When she turns to look up at me, I see warm caramel eyes blink behind thick black lashes as she looks at me curiously.

Waving my hand toward the missing chunk of her dress, she catches on.

"Oh, yeah, that would be good, thanks." Her voice goes bashful and a pretty blush tints her cheeks.

Chapter Three

Violet

The fabric of my dress is still kinda slimy from Alfred making it his lunch, but I hang on to it for dear life anyway.

I'd forgotten all about how much of my skin was on display when I saw the alpacas and now that the burly mountain man has reminded me about it, I'm feeling self-conscious again.

"So what's your name, anyway?" His dark whiskey voice floats on the afternoon breeze over his shoulder as I follow him toward the cabin.

"Violet," I answer.

He holds the door open for me and I get my first look at his home.

It's a weathered log cabin built in a long ranch house style with a board porch and an overhang of eaves covering it, held up with thick posts.

The porch has rocking chairs on either side of a

table made of a roughly finished wooden slab with live edges. As if someone had merely put a tree through a meat slicer.

"My brother made it," he mentions when he sees me eyeing it. The way he says it sounds almost defensive.

"It's cool," I say, "I like that the board still has all the rough edges."

The interior of the cabin is, frankly, more than I'd expected.

The walls are the bare logs that make up the outside of the house, that much I'd expected, but the floor is made of angular slabs of slate, covered by thick braided rugs in the living area.

A big, stone fireplace takes up the entire wall on one end of the main room with comfortable-looking furniture gathered near it in the way that modern homes in the city gather their furniture around big screen TVs.

There's not a television in sight in here though.

On the other end of the main room is a country kitchen with butcher block counter-tops wrapping around the entire space and a dining table made in the same live edge fashion as the little table on the porch sitting in the center of the space.

On the living room side, cut into the back wall, an over-sized doorway appears to lead to a hallway.

"My brother's getting married to a gal who's got a cousin named Violet," his voice booms from a room somewhere beyond that hall.

"Apparently she helped clear up some mysteries in

our family history," he goes on, emerging from the back of the house with a flannel shirt that's sure to be considerably longer than my sundress.

"It's probably too warm for this," he tells me, as he thrusts the shirt toward me, his arm outstretched from a distance as if he's afraid of getting too close to me, "but it'll cover ya."

"Thanks," I step closer than is strictly necessary to take the shirt from his hand.

I want to be in his space, letting the scent of him fill my nose and enjoying the way he makes me feel dizzy and hot.

"Is Birch your brother?" I ask, slipping the flannel over my dress.

He slips back into what I can see now is a large bedroom at the end of the hall just behind the doorway. I inhale the scent of his shirt deeply.

It's all clean cotton and line-dried sunshine and mountain air. I'm sure it's what he would smell like if I'd run into him down in town somewhere, but it's lacking the masculine aroma of sweat and soil that has had me feeling flushed and needy since he first stepped into my personal space to grab Alfred.

Beyond the doorway of the big bedroom, I hear the sound of a shower running and almost as quickly being turned off.

Inching closer to invading the privacy of his room, I check out the place where this man sleeps at night.

A bed that's more than big enough for his size is up

against the far wall. Windows on either side of the headboard. The room doesn't have a proper closet, just a long pole running across the room next the to the bed with acres of flannel and denim hanging from it. Boots line the floor beneath.

The sound of him showering quickly comes from a doorway opposite the bed and I'm dangerously close to peeking through the open door when he emerges unexpectedly, not quite wearing a towel.

"Oh, sorry," I jump back out of the bedroom, back into the hall.

Behind me I hear a gruff chuckle.

"Yeah, Birch is my brother," he answers my last question. "So you must be Maggie's cousin then?"

When he joins me back in the living room, he's put on fresh jeans and a t-shirt strains over that beautiful chest I'd been fantasizing about licking.

"Sorry for leaving you out here like that." He runs his hand up the back of his neck and gives me a bashful look that seems out of character for the rough looking man. "Thought I'd wash the goat off me real quick."

"So you must be Cypress?" I nod in understanding when he tells me about the quick shower and even though I'm disappointed that he put on a shirt, honestly? It's probably for the better. At least I can almost put two thoughts together now that I'm not staring at all that delicious man real estate he had on display earlier.

In answer to my question I get a grunt from him as

he opens the door of the refrigerator and pulls out a pitcher of sweet tea.

Cypress is the mystery McAllister. An enigmatic recluse living up on the mountain away from town. His own family doesn't know much about him outside of not being much for people.

Maggie's met him. She says he's come down to join them for the weekly family dinners maybe twice since she's been with Birch. She told me that Birch told her not to make plans to include Cypress in the wedding party because they'll be lucky if he shows up at all. There's no way he'd be comfortable getting dressed up and walking down the aisle with a stranger to stand up in front of half the town while they say their vows.

That's why I'll be doing my maid of honor walk solo next weekend.

As I watch the big man filling two glasses with tea, I'm suddenly disappointed.

Cypress

"So what brought you all the way up here this morning all dressed up like a summer dream?"

I hand her a glass of tea and lead her back out onto the porch, figuring it'll be less temptation for me that way. Having her here inside the cabin has me spun up something crazy.

"We did pictures this morning," she tells me, looking at me like I should know that already, "family photos for Birch and Maggie's wedding."

Frowning over my tea glass I stare out into the field I was working on this morning. Yeah, that's right. Somewhere in the back of my mind I seem to remember something about someone saying they were getting together this week up at the resort. There were supposed to be family pictures and general McAllister mayhem that's going to serve as bachelor and bachelorette parties combined if I recall.

I give Violet a grunt because I think she's waiting for me to respond but honestly? My family wasn't expecting me to be in those pictures. Hell, Birch already let me know he and Maggie won't be upset if I don't show for the wedding.

The clan knows I'm not much for spending time around people.

I make it down to see them every so often.

Still. If I hung around more, I'd have met my little mint cupcake sooner. We'd have gotten to know each other months ago and I wouldn't be sitting here rocking on my front porch trying to act civilized when my dick is so hard that even the burst of ice cold shower water couldn't bring it more than halfway down.

If I'd met Violet when she first came up and met the rest of my family, she'd be mine already. I'd know every dip and curve of that sweet body of hers. I know what her nectar tastes like and the sweet sounds she makes when she comes for me.

We wouldn't be sitting six feet apart from each other sipping sweet tea like a couple of old grannies. She'd be naked in my bed right now with my cock filling her up with my seed.

The notion hits me out of the blue and I choke on my tea. Never in nearly forty years on this earth have I had the urge to breed a woman but inside of an hour of knowing Violet, my head is filling up with all kinds of crazy ideas.

When I think of the time I've already lost with this precious angel I'm filled with sense of regret that I'm not used to. I imagine if she was truly mine, living up here with me and the animals, doing whatever it is that makes her happy while I'm out working the land. What it would be like to come inside and sink my cock into that voluptuous body of hers whenever I get the urge. How it'd be to watch her belly grow round with my child. All the years we'd have together to chase goats and babies-- and each other-- around this mountain.

Instead of playing polite host with sweet tea and conversation like we are right now.

"Are you OK?"

Violet's standing beside me, patting me on the back while I choke on the tea and my own misguided imagination.

"I'm fine, sweetheart," I grunt out, "gonna take more

than a sip of tea going down the wrong pipe to do me in."

Her little hand is still against my back, and her touch has me lit up like a live wire.

"So how come you don't spend more time with your family?" she asks me and that's enough to bring all those thoughts that were running away with me right back down to earth.

Catching her around her waist, I pull her down on my lap just like I've been wanting to, and wrap my hand around her thigh right where Alfred's bite mark gives me access to her smooth skin.

I'm surprised when she lets me, settling across my thighs like she's waiting for me to tell her a story and just like that, my dick is straining at my zipper again.

"Surprised one of my asshole brothers hasn't already filled you in," I chide, letting my fingertips drag over her flesh and taking pride in the way the goosebumps rise up and her nipples poke against that ruffled up fabric so close to my face now that it'd be all too easy to skip the personal history lesson and just pull one into my mouth.

Violet wiggles against my legs, twisting slightly so she's facing me more and I can feel the heat of her pussy on my thigh.

"They just say they don't get to see you much," she says.

"Well you've met the clan, you know our roots run deep here on the ridge."

Violet nods, those curls of hers shimmying around her shoulders and that hot little space between her legs rocking against mine in a way that makes it damn hard to concentrate on anything else.

"Well, I was the one that wanted to see the world. Joined the Army right out of high school. Jumped through their hoops, took all their tests, ended up wearing a green beret."

Violet's hazel eyes widen, her lips making an adorable little *O*.

"Thought I was going to make a career out of it till a bad jump left me with a broken spine and a limp I can't hide when it rains."

"Oh," she gasps, her arm snaking around my neck as I talk, "that had to be hard."

"In the end, I didn't have a choice. I spent a few months in hospitals and rehab learning how to walk again but they wouldn't clear me to return to active duty. So an honorable discharge and a Purple Heart later and I was back in Moonshine Ridge but after all that I discovered even the ridge was too much noise and bustle for me. So I packed up and moved back up here. It's my great great great granddaddy Brodie's original homestead."

"It's in amazing shape for being that old," her eyes scan the house.

"I did a lot of work on the place," I assure her. "Added the bedrooms, and the plumbing. Set up the solar for the electric. Bought a breeding pair of alpacas and built the farm.

"Truth is, sweetheart," I look up and search her soft eyes, "It took a long time for me to get anywhere near being right again in the head and now I'm just not much good to anyone. Old Alfred out there is better company than I am."

Chapter Four

Violet

"I think you're perfect company, Cypress."

My voice sounds so sure of itself I barely even recognize it as my own. I stare into his eyes, all deep moss and stormy seas right now and then my eyes drop to his lips; full, firm, and tempting surrounded by beard and mustache that I'm dying to feel against me.

I don't know who the brazen girl is that's leaning in to kiss him now, but when his lips meet mine, I'm grateful that she showed up.

What else am I brave enough to do, I wonder?

Cypress's arm wraps around my shoulder, the hand that's been idly laying on my thigh grips tighter and moves higher, pulling me onto him fully till I can feel the ridge of his hard manhood pressing into my thigh.

His lips are commanding, his tongue insistent at the seam of mine till I open for him. Taking cues from him,

I let my tongue slide against his, teasing, tangling, and then I get brave and nip at his lower lip.

His fingers dig into my leg and he attacks my mouth with a vengeance, stroking his tongue against mine in an obscene rhythm that has me scrambling to rearrange myself over his lap.

Straddling him now, I can push my pussy down against that hard ridge and feel it dig into my mound.

"You like that?" Cypress pulls from my lips so he can watch my eyes roll into the back of my head when he rolls his hips so that I can feel him even more completely. "You like feeling how hard my cock is for you?"

"Yes," I answer him, "I love feeling how hard you are."

There's that brazen girl again, stealing my thoughts and speaking them aloud for me.

My hands are wrapped in his t-shirt as I pull him to kiss me again. Then I'm trying to touch all of him at once, my hands running under his shirt feeling that chest that was on display for me not so long ago, then reaching between us and popping the button on his jeans.

"Careful, sweetheart," he growls, "you sure you know what you're doing?"

His voice is gruff and it holds a dark promise behind his words but I have to take a deep breath. Looking up at him, straight into those eyes that have gone so dark they're nearly black now, I shake my head in a honest answer.

"I have no idea what I'm doing, Cypress," I admit shyly, all traces of that bold girl gone now, "but I want to taste you. Please."

His hands thread in my hair, wrapping around my head as he pulls me in for another kiss. This one deep and tender.

"You can do anything you want with me, baby," he whispers against my lips softly. "But don't think you have to."

My hands already have his zipper down and his huge erection out.

Shimmying off his lap, I lower myself to my knees on the boards of the porch, fitting between his thighs as he widens them to allow me space.

He's so hard, like a steel pole but his skin here is so soft at the same time. I'm completely fascinated and when I test the right grip with a firm stroke along his length, Cypress grabs the arms of the rocking chair with a white knuckled grip, his hips coming up off the seat in a sudden jerk.

I love how sensitive he is, how I can make him sigh and groan with just the way I move my hand, and when I lean forward and slide my tongue over the wet slit of his dick to lap at the bead of salty precum there, the string of curse words that he lets loose has me feeling brave again.

Sealing my lips around his broad head, I let my

hands slide down and do my best to take as much of him as I can in my mouth. Sucking and swirling my tongue along the delicate underside of him as I go, loving every grunted curse and moan he utters as I do it.

I experiment with my grip, I try licking him from the bottom to the tip, I slide my tongue through the slit at the top and moan at the taste of him.

Then his hands are in my hair again, his hips bucking under me and I can feel the swell and surge as he gets close.

Part of me is nervous, knowing what I'm committing to only in theory, but I want it. I want to taste all of him.

"Violet, baby girl, you need to stop or I'm going to come down your pretty little throat."

His words are coarse and ground out like it hurts him to talk, but his warning does nothing to deter me.

"Is that what you want, sweetheart?" His voice is husky. I nod around his dick without taking my mouth off him.

A sharp exhale makes his stomach jump and twitch under the heel of my hand.

"You want me to come in your mouth, baby? You gonna drink me down if I do that?"

Cypress

. . .

This girl. She hums happily on my cock and works my shaft with a determined fist. I'm making a knotted mess of her hair and I'm fucking her sweet mouth roughly but she never lets go.

I want to hear her say it and I'm about to command her to tell me when I look down and see her eyes on mine, her swollen lips sliding over my skin as she smiles around my dick and then I fucking lose control, pumping ropes of cum down her throat and growling like a mad man while she takes everything I give her without spilling a drop.

Violet smacks her lips and runs her tongue over my deflating cock one more time for good measure before climbing back up in my lap.

"Good girl," I tell her softly, rubbing her back and kissing her, "you sure you never did that before?"

Her curls dance around her head as it shakes back and forth. "It was OK then?"

"Fuck yeah," I smooth my hand down her tangled hair, "it was better than OK."

There's only one thought left on my mind now, and that's that I need to get this girl into my bed.

Awkwardly tucking myself back together, I pick her up as I stand, lifting her by the backs of her thighs so her legs wrap around my waist, the heat of her pussy as it bounces against me bringing my dick back to attention as I rush us inside and throw her down on the middle of my bed.

"My turn," I growl.

Grabbing her ankles and dragging her ass down to the edge of the bed, I fall to my knees between those thick thighs that are splayed wide for me and yank those little lace panties that have been teasing me down her legs.

When the scrap of lace is free in my hand, I bury my nose in the damp center of the fabric and inhale her scent. Then I turn my attention to the source.

Her sweet pussy is swollen with need and flushed a deep rose, already glistening and wet for me. My reawakened member pulses with the need to claim this woman, to make her mine completely but my greedy dick has to wait.

I need to make my angel come with my face between her legs.

With one hand wrapped around her thigh I push my shoulders farther between her knees and get my first taste. Dragging my tongue along her slit I lap up her juices with a groan.

Violet's thighs shudder under my hands, her breath catching and making her stomach quiver as I breathe her in, tracing her folds and memorizing every contour, every place that makes her squirm or jump or moan.

Using my fingers to spread her wide, I lick from her hole to her clit and enjoy Violet's soft whimper. When I slip the pad of my fingertip against her opening, I can see the ring of thin flesh that still guards her entrance. The sight of her intact cherry has my breath coming ragged, my need to make her mine even stronger.

"Violet," I manage to find my voice, commanding her to answer me, "tell me the truth, baby--" I look up from the mesmerizing sight of her innocent pussy as it clenches around my first knuckle begging for more. "-- Has any other man been in this pretty little pussy before me?"

She raises her head off the mattress to stare down at me. The little green dress bunched up around her waist, my other hand splayed out over the swell of her belly with my thumb brushing the dark, damp curls covering her mound.

"If I say no, are you going to stop?"

My girl's got a wicked side to her and if I wasn't fighting with every ounce of strength in my body to slow the fuck down and take my time with her right now, I might laugh.

"Fuck no, sweetheart," I growl, "this is mine."

Violet's head falls back with a soft thud and a moan. My finger slides in deep, careful not to rupture that thin sheath of skin. I'm going to do that properly when I take her with my cock for the first time. Right now, I want her coming on my tongue, I want her cream saturating my beard as she rides my face while I make her scream for me.

And that's what I make her do for me now. Crooking my finger inside her and stroking the bundle of nerves against her inner wall while I suck her clit till Violet's a writhing, wild thing rumpling my sheets.

Her heels dig into my back and her thighs tighten on my neck. She's rocking against my face and pulling at my hair while her screams echo off the mountains.

I don't stop till she goes limp, then I change the hard suction against her sensitive clit to soft kisses and when I slip my drenched finger from her channel I clean her juices off with my mouth.

Fuck she's perfect.

My cock is aching to take her. To claim her. To brand her with my seed and bind her to me, but I can see she needs a break..

Kissing my way back up to her lips, I will my cock to be patient and pull her into my arms while I lay beside her.

"I was hoping you weren't going to stop there," she murmurs drowsily as she snuggles against my chest.

"When I pop that cherry I want you begging for my cock, not so tuckered out you sleep through it."

Chapter Five

Violet

He makes me laugh. There's no way I could sleep through it if it feels anything like what he just did to me. But it does feel good to rest, cradled in Cypress's protective arms while his lips drop soft kisses along the crown of my head while his steady heartbeat thuds against my ear.

I can't remember when I've ever felt safer.

The breeze blows through the open windows, billowing the curtains and bringing in the warm, clean scents of the mountain. Birds sing somewhere outside. I hear a squirrel chittering in a tree, soft bleats from the goats in their pen and then a crash that sounds like it came from the master bath.

Cypress is up in a flash placing his body between me and the source of the noise.

"Stay put," he orders before he stalks toward the door of the bathroom where more noises indicate that something is definitely in there. Destroying things, from the sound of it.

"Alfred!"

Cypress lunges but the wily goat manages to scamper past him. Hooves slipping on the hard floor and then he's a blur of brown and white as the sound of his bell follows him out the front door.

I sit in the center of Cypress's big bed and laugh uncontrollably.

"Damn goat," Cypress mutters as he stomps around the bathroom picking up whatever Alfred broke.

"That's what I get for not closing the door." He grins at me. "Someone had me too distracted."

He looks at me with a glint in his eye that has my pulse thrumming between my legs but when I see the clock on his night stand I'm scrambling to get myself together.

"Shit, is that clock right?" I pull his flannel back over my torn dress and search the floor for my panties and the sandals that got kicked off somewhere between his orgasm and mine.

"Yeah. Why? What's wrong? You gotta hot date in town?"

He's joking, but I can see the dark possessiveness in his eyes that says he's also not joking.

"Job interview." I'm quick to clear up. "Video call this afternoon, I have to get all the way back down to Keller's Ferry."

A shadow flickers across Cypress's handsome face

Finding the Mountain Man

and for a moment I think he's going to forbid me from leaving. That he might actually insist that I stay here with him.

"Video interview? Where's the job then?" He asks when his features clear.

Just thinking about the job makes my stomach curl. Especially after today, now that I've met Cypress.

My voice drops with my mood. "Portland," I whisper while I drag my sandals back on.

"Oregon?"

His voice notches up and I nod.

"Here, wear this," he thrusts a pair of sweat pants and one of his t-shirts at me. "You're not going into Keller's in half a dress and no underwear."

"I don't get my panties back?"

Our moods lighten again, me with a fist on one hip giving him an accusatory smirk while he pulls my panties from his back pocket, makes a show of sniffing them and grins.

"Nope."

Cypress walks me down the drive, back to my car.

"You drive safe," he tells me for the millionth time. He leans across me and buckles me in before I can do it for myself.

"You come back as soon as you can, Violet. We're not done."

His lips bruise mine with a rough kiss before he stands up and closes my door after making sure I'm safely all the way inside.

Rocklyn Ryder

Cypress

I watch her car roll away and I manage to keep it together till she's completely out of sight before I start to lose my mind.

Portland, Oregon is closer than Portland, Maine but it's a long fucking way from Moonshine Ridge. I knew it, knew it when I laid eyes on her; that she was the kind of girl who needs the thrum and pulse of a city.

What do I have to offer her? A hard cock, a warm bed. Mornings that start before dawn to take care of the animals, lazy afternoons of sipping tea on the front porch rocking chairs, going down to the ridge once a month to pick up the few things I can't produce for myself here on the farm, checking in on Nan, dinner with my folks on occasion.

A small town life and that's all.

I was a fool to let my head get filled up with ideas of making Violet my wife and spending the rest of my days filling this land up with babies to chase instead of goats.

I spent the afternoon patching the fence around the goat pen, hunting down all of Alfred's secret trap doors and sealing his escape routes.

Goats get fed. Alpacas get secured. I clean up the

mess Alfred made by sneaking into the house while I was busy making Violet come for me.

Fuck! I can still taste her sweet pussy. I still have her coating my beard.

Sun sets late this time of year and by night fall I've even managed to rip up most of that field I was working on. By the time I'm working with nothing but starlight I've run out of chores to keep me busy.

The cold shower isn't enough to keep my hand off my dick. When I get out and get dressed, it kills me that I don't smell like her anymore.

Stuffing her stolen panties back in my pocket, just for the feeling of having her close again, I know I've about gone mad.

I skipped dinner and I've got no interest in eating it.

I need Violet back.

Why did I let her leave? I should have told her she belongs to me now. Should have claimed her properly, filled her with my seed and made it clear that this is her home now.

She doesn't need a job as long as she's with me. I'll take care of her. If she wants to work, then I sure as hell know enough people down in Moonshine Ridge to find her a job if helping me around the farm and riding my cock isn't enough to keep her busy.

My thoughts start to spin out of control along with my patience. What if something happened to her? What if she hit a deer on the way down the mountain? What if she ran into trouble down in Keller's Ferry?

It's not a bad place but it's got more than a few bars for a town its size and last I heard, it was caught up in a turf war between a couple of motorcycle clubs that had moved into the area.

Why haven't I ever installed phone lines up here? Gotten some damn satellite internet, some way to make a call or get a hold of someone in an emergency?

Violet could be in trouble.

Yanking the cabin door open with the keys to my truck in the other hand I've got one foot over the threshold on my way to hunt her down. I need to know she's safe.

I need my girl back on my mountain with me.

Chapter Six

Violet

My body still buzzes from the memory of our afternoon.

His deep voice telling me telling me to come back plays on an endless loop in my head.

There's no way to call him. I can't text or send an email. His cabin is completely off the grid up there and even if he has a cell phone, there's no service up at his place.

That's actually the reason I'm down in Keller's Ferry instead of staying in Moonshine Ridge. Even in the dead center of town, cell signal is iffy up there and the internet gets knocked out easily every time a storm passes through-- which is often, even in the late summer. With my job search, I needed to make sure I had reliable internet access.

What if I drove back up there? Tonight. Right now.

Will he be surprised when someone's knocking on

his door well after dark? What will he think when he opens the door and sees me standing on his porch?

Did he really mean it when he said I was welcome to come back? Was it just the thing he was thinking at that moment, or would he be happy to see me.

Would he take me back to his bed and finish what we started this afternoon?

Could I really drive back up the mountain tonight to ask a man I just met to make love to me? Am I that brave?

It's a long drive back up to the ridge in the light of day, at night I have to take the curves extra slow and keep my eyes peeled for deer or other animals crossing the road. And Cypress's driveway is well beyond the sleeping town of Moonshine Ridge.

This time I drive up the steep grade that winds around the contours of the mountain until leveling out in the graveled circular drive in front of Cypress's cabin.

Just as I'm slamming the car door shut and heading for the porch, his front door opens and Cypress's huge bulk blocks the light from within the cabin as he steps outside.

He's so handsome. Everything inside me turns to liquid when his harsh glare goes soft as soon as he sees it's me.

I want this man forever, but if this week is all we have I don't want to miss it.

Finding the Mountain Man

Cypress

She's here.

The air goes out of my lungs and for a second I stand on my own front porch and forget to breathe. Then I rush toward her, grabbing her up in my arms and easily carrying her inside to my bed-- remembering to kick the front door shut this time.

"Did you miss me, sweetheart?" I growl in her ear as I pull the long t-shirt type dress over her head and unhook her bra.

Violet giggles at my eagerness but nods as she gets busy with the buttons on my shirt.

"Yeah, I missed you," she says.

The way she says it is a little shy, like she's sharing a secret with me. That and the breathless sound of her voice go straight to my dick.

I was hard the second I saw her car sitting in my drive, but now the fucker surges like it's trying to break though the denim of my jeans and lunge for her.

Her unfettered tits are perfection, full and heavy, with large areolas and nipples elongated and puckered, filling my hands to overflowing. When I lean in to pull one in to my mouth, Violet topples backward on the mattress.

My weight lands over her, my hips settling into the

bedding between her thighs while I keep giving her breasts the attention they deserve.

I know I'm bigger than her, heavy on top of her and maybe I should be shifting to take some of my weight off her but I like having her pinned under me like this. The ways her little hands manage to push my shirt off of my shoulders, the way her curvy body wiggles up against mine like she needs me even closer.

There's only way I can get closer to her than I am already am right now, and if she doesn't stop moving around under me like this, she's going to find out how much closer we can get.

"Baby, you're making me crazy with you squirming like that," I grind out around the hard nipple I have between my teeth. She wiggles again and I bite down. Just enough to warn her that she's got a half feral man on top of her-- she should think carefully about the consequences of her actions.

Violet gasps, arching her back. Her hands go scrabbling between us again, pushing down into the waistband of my jeans and brushing those soft little fingertips against the swollen head of my dick.

Her touch has me seeing stars, cursing against her silky flesh. My hips press forward, trying to put some pressure against my hard-on, just enough to slow down the need to thrust wildly into her hand as it wraps around my girth.

"Fuck baby," I grit out, moving up her body to kiss

her like my life depends on it. "You got me too wound up, I'm not going to be able to wait much longer."

"I don't want you to wait," she whispers. Her hands undo my jeans and I shuck 'em off in a second flat, my boxer briefs join them another second later as Violet uses her foot to drag them down my legs.

"Limber little minx, ain't ya?" I chuckle at the way she wrapped her legs around me to get me naked but knowing she can bend like that has all kinds of filthy images filling my head.

"Yoga," she tells me.

There's nothing left between us but her panties now, and I line up and press my hard length into her mound, right up against her slit, just to torture us both.

Violet's head presses back into my pillows, her eyes fluttering half closed as she breathes out a choked little gasp that only makes me surge harder against her.

"Baby--" I kiss her breasts, I kiss the swell of her stomach and the dip of her waist, and lick across the edge of her hip bone as I work my way down her body so I can drip my noise into the new pair of panties she's brought for my growing collection.

Sporty little hiphuggers this time, soft gray cotton with a wide pink elastic band. That gray cotton shows up dark in the middle where she's drenched and ready for me.

"--Violet, baby," I call up at my girl softly from where I'm rubbing the pad of my thumb against her wet center.

She finally lifts her head and stares down at me, the fire in her warm hazel eyes making me thrust my cock into the mattress under me. My fingers slide under the edge of her panties, spreading her moisture through her swollen sex and then I let one finger slip all the way inside.

"--Earlier, when I was down here," I kiss the inside of her thigh, "I noticed you're still in tact."

She props up on her elbows, her eyes losing that lust daze I like seeing in them when she's looking at me. I'll put it back though. I just need to make sure first.

"Wh-what do you mean?"

Licking my lips and giving her a grin, I trace the edge of her innocence with the pointed tip of my tongue, that thin film of skin standing between the outside world and heaven.

"It's your first time, isn't it, baby?" I ask, pressing past and making her moan. "I'm going to be the first man who's been inside you, won't I?"

"You can tell?" She sounds sad about it, like something's wrong with her. The urge to pull her into my arms and comfort her rides me hard but the need to claim her and make her mine is even stronger.

"In your case, I can," I say gently, "you sure about this, Vi?"

I scramble up her body and cover it with my own, pinning her hips with mine and using my knees to wedge her thighs open wider.

"I'm sure, Cypress," she whispers up at me, "I want it to be you."

There's no more restraint left in me. Whatever other conversations we oughta be having are forgotten before I'm even past her resistance.

She's so wet for me, I slip past her entrance easily before it takes effort to push farther into her virgin tunnel.

I'm a selfish asshole for not being gentler with her, but I need to feel her around all of me, need to have her walls squeezing my cock and know what it feels like to finally be *home*.

Violet's nails dig into my shoulders, her heels in the backs of my thighs.

"Ow," she cried out sharply just as I feel her body give way and open up for me.

"Sorry, sweetheart." I feel like shit when I see her face pinched with the pain. I'm a rough bastard and I don't deserve the gift she's giving me. It takes everything I have to force myself to be still for her, but Violet's a fucking treasure and I'll be damned if I'm going to put my needs ahead of hers no matter how much effort it takes.

"We can stop if you want," I whisper hoarsely against her ear, praying she doesn't prove me a liar.

Chapter Seven

Violet

"The fuck we can."

My voice is all air, my heart's beating a mile a minute, and I can feel the soreness where he ripped through my virginity but the feeling of being full with him inside me far out-shadows the slight sting.

Kicking Cypress in his gloriously hard glutes like a horse that I want to go faster, I reach around his neck and pull his face to mine.

"Don't you dare stop, Cypress McAllister."

With my feet pulled up so high, my hips tilt back, opening me up for him even more.

Cypress slides inside me all the way to the root of his thick cock. I can feel my body stretching to accommodate him while he holds still to let me adjust.

"OK," I pant under him, "that's good. I'm going to need you to fuck me properly now."

I don't have to tell him twice.

Cypress growls then kisses me. His hips pull back and the absence of him where I'd felt so complete seconds before has me keening in protest as my body instinctively follows his. Then he brings it back to me, thrusting fast and slamming into me with force again and again.

Sweat beads on my skin and drips from Cypress's chest as the wet sounds of our bodies moving together fills the quiet cabin and the mountains around us.

My body doesn't hurt anymore, it feels alive and so good, and then I feel the sensation building. I need more of him, I need him deeper to bring that feeling closer.

"Fuck baby," he groans into my throat, "you're so close, I can feel it."

Cypress pushes his hand between us and hits my clit with the pad of his thumb.

"Come for me sweetheart, come on my cock like a good girl." His voice is a dark rasp from somewhere above me and then I can feel my insides grabbing at him just as hard as my hands are grabbing at his hips.

"Fuck Violet, I'm not going to make it through that. You feel too fucking good coming on my cock so hard."

Cypress pulls his head back and roars his release above me, chasing me over the precipice as he releases jets of his hot liquid cum deep inside me.

When I pry myself out of Cypress's bed in the morning, I'm sore in ways that make me smile remembering our night together and being woken up twice more by Cypress's very insistent cock.

"Hey beautiful," Cypress is standing at the stove flipping pancakes when I join him in the kitchen after a long, hot shower. "How's my girl this morning?"

He's wearing pajamas pants and an apron. I never knew a spatula could be so sexy till now.

"Good," I stand on my tip-toes to meet his lips halfway for a kiss. "How's my sexy mountain man?"

A deep noise comes out of his throat that almost sounds like purring-- if bears, for instance, purred. I give him a smack on his ass when he leans down to catch my earlobe between his teeth.

"Keep it up and I'm going to have you again right here on the kitchen counter," he tells me.

That is a threat that I strongly consider pushing my luck on before ducking out of his reach, taking a plate of golden cakes with me.

"I have to get back down the mountain," I tell him, sadness clouding my happy morning.

"Hell yeah we do," Cypress surprises me so much by agreeing that I don't notice he said "we" at first. He sits on the chair at the table beside me and makes a sloppy show of licking the syrup off my lips. "We're going to get you out of that place you're renting and move you in here with me. Why are you down there anyway? Instead of staying up on the ridge with Birch and Maggie?"

One look up from my breakfast and he gives a hearty laugh. Nodding, he tells me he gets it.

Birch and Maggie can't keep their hands off each other in public, spending the night under the same roof with them isn't the quietest night I've ever spent. I usually get a room at the lodge.

"How come you're not there this time then?"

"I had to have reliable internet for the job interview." I shrug, not really wanting to spoil my good mood talking about that.

His face darkens as he finished his breakfast.

"But that's over, right? You did your interview? How'd it go?"

Using cleaning up as an excuse to avoid letting him see my face, I take plates to the sink.

"Good. I think," I answer as he joins me at the sink.

Side by side, we wash and dry and put away and it feels so-- nice. Doing this trivial domestic chore with him. For a moment I let myself imagine what life could be like if I could stay up here with Cypress. Spending our days together taking care of the cooking and cleaning and working side by side to take care of the farm as well.

Something hits the window nearest us and Cypress breaks into another deep belly laugh when I nearly jump out of my skin as Alfred headbutts the window again.

Finding the Mountain Man

Cypress

Guess I didn't fix all his escape routes after all.

"Is he going to break the window?" Violet asks.

"Not anymore, I put in half inch plexi on those lower panes two years ago after he broke through for the third time."

After I find Violet some of my clothes to wear, she joins me outside, learning how the farm works while I feed goats and alpacas and open the gate so the alpacas can graze in the big pasture.

It's nice having her out here with me. I'm looking forward to the life I'm planning on having with her by my side when she has to go and remind me about the damn job she's chasing.

"I'm just waiting to hear back," she tells me, patting Alfred on the head and making sure he doesn't eat more clothes, "they said they'd be in touch by the end of the week."

"Wedding's this weekend ain't it?"

"Rehearsal on Friday, are you coming?"

"Not gonna miss it if it's where you'll be," I lift her hand to my lips and give her a wink.

"So there's no reason for you to stay down in Keller's now. You can get a message from the ridge. Let's go get you out of that place, you're gonna stay with me as long as you're up here."

Violet smiles and climbs up into the cab of my truck when I hold the door open for her. I love that she's not arguing with me. Now if only I could manage to hope she'll be half as cooperative if I tell her not to take this damn job.

"Paralegal," she answers when I ask her what it is she does anyway.

That's a fancy job. I was hoping she was a barista or maybe decorated cakes or something. Something she could do up here with a little figuring it out. I don't think there's much call for paralegal services up in Moonshine Ridge.

"You'll get it," I tell her, sliding her hand over to my thigh and covering it with my own as we wind down the mountain road. "They'd be fools not to hire you."

We spend the day getting her moved out of the little place she's been renting and back into my place.

She promises me she's not too sore for me to have her again in the afternoon after the farm chores are done and Alfred's pen has been repaired again. When I try to go slow for her, she pushes me back and rides me like a Valkyrie.

This girl's got me tied in knots around her finger already.

Violet's still young. Sixteen years my junior. She went to school for her professional credentials, she plans on having a career and in order to do that, she needs to be in a city where there's plenty of work for her and big name legal firms to build her resume on.

I doing my best to be supportive but inside I'm a wreck counting down the days I have left with her, facing the agonizing choices that I'll have to make when she's ready to leave the ridge.

Chapter Eight

Violet

The wedding rehearsal went smoothly, considering the last minute changes now that Cypress has agreed to walk down the aisle with me. Not that there were any complaints about him joining the wedding party.

Birch and Maggie were both ecstatic that he showed up tonight and will be in the ceremony tomorrow-- and at the reception. As long as he's with me, he says.

I wouldn't have it any other way. I may not get to keep him forever, but as long I'm with him, he's mine and I don't want to let him out of my sight for an instant.

Cedar closed the tavern early for the rehearsal dinner tonight. Now the entire McAllister clan and a few close friends of the family are all scattered throughout the dining room of the tavern laughing, drinking, and swapping tall tales about Moonshine Ridge and their family histories here.

Even Cypress is laughing and talking shit with his brothers, refusing to give baby Rose up to anyone else, and never straying too far from me.

Damn, he looks good with a baby in his arms. He's a natural with her. My lower belly pulls with desire and I'm pretty sure my ovaries are on fire.

My phone buzzes in my pocket letting me know I have a new message and shaking me out of my daydreams. Looking at the screen, I tap Cypress's arm and let him know I'm just stepping away to listen to the voicemail and I'll be right back.

He leans down past Rose's sweet baby face to give me a kiss and I wish this could be us forever.

If Cypress asked, I'd stay. I don't even have to think twice about that, I knew the second I found him up on his mountain that I belonged with him. But he's been nothing but supportive about this job opportunity, encouraging me to pursue my dreams and reach for my goals.

If only he knew how far from Portland, or any other city, my dreams really are.

After listening to the message twice, anything that felt like hope has slithered out of me and all that's left is despair.

Inside the tavern, the sounds of love and laughter make me feel all the more alone suddenly. I can't go back in yet. All I can do is slide down the side of the building till I'm crumpled in a heap on the ground and cry.

Cypress

Is this really the first time I've held my niece?

At only nine weeks old, little Rose is tiny in my big old hands but every time someone reaches for her, I find myself refusing to give her up.

She looks up at me with big eyes, her angel soft hair almost the same red as her mama's sticking up in every direction as she tries to take in the whole world around her at once.

I need one of these. Hell, I need six of these. A half dozen wide-eyed little dolls with their mama's eyes and dark skin to show the world to.

Part of me is more than hoping that I've already put a baby in Violet's belly. I want to watch her grow with my child and make a family of our own together, but I'd be lying if I pretended I wouldn't also be overjoyed for an excuse to keep her here with me.

Tonight has been an eye-opener. Looking around at my clan, all laughing and talking and telling stories and lies, I realize how much I've been missing out on by keeping to myself so much.

All three of my baby brothers have women of their own now. Ash and Hyacinth have been hitched for damn near a year already. Never thought it'd be the youngest of us boys to give Mom and Dad their first grandbaby, but here she is, dosing off in my arms.

And when did Cedar stop kidding himself about his feelings for Chamomile? The girl he hired as a waitress earlier this summer and then acted like he couldn't stand her while we all saw him pining for her the whole time. They're here tonight, glued to each other everywhere they go.

Nan's in a booth talking shit and drinking whiskey with Marcia-- I better not end up with another goat after tonight.

Nan's always been tough as nails and larger than life in my eyes, even though she's a wisp of a woman at barely over five foot tall and a hundred pounds soaking wet, but tonight it's like I'm seeing her for the first time in ages. She's gotta be in her early 80s now.

Shit, Mom and Dad aren't getting any younger either.

After the time I did in the service, I should know how fragile life is. How quickly it can be lost. And I've been missing it. Missing out on all this, on the time I have with the people I love.

Reluctantly, I hand a sleeping Rose over to her mother.

I need to find my girl. Here or some crowded city, it doesn't matter, I need Violet with me and it's time I made sure she understands that.

It takes me more than a few tries before I find her and when I do, my heart is crushed. She's sitting on the cold concrete outside the kitchen door, her knees bent and her tear-streaked face smashed against them with her arms wrapped around her legs.

"Violet, sweetheart, come here," I sit down beside her and gather her up in my lap. "Baby, what happened? Did they give the job to someone else?"

She tucks her head under my chin and I feel her curls bouncing against my chest as she shakes her head.

"They want me to start next week." She sniffles.

Shit. For a second there, I'd been hoping it had fallen through.

"Baby, I'm confused," I tell her, pulling her chin up to get her to look at me, "if you got the job, why are you so upset?"

That's when she lays it out for me and I realize I've been misunderstanding this whole time. Violet confesses that she hates city life. In fact, she's been having panic attacks ever since she started her job search.

She'd hoped to find work in a small town-- a town like Moonshine Ridge-- and buy a small place with the money she got from an inheritance when her grandfather passed away but the housing market has been out of control and jobs are scarce in communities like the ridge.

"I witnessed a woman get attacked when I was fourteen," she quietly confesses, "I had to give a report to the police and everything and I always remember the officer saying that things like that happen in cities. He said it like it was no big deal but I never felt safe in the city after that. I never wanted to live in the city again. Any city."

Well hell.

I hold her tight and smooth her hair along her back while she burrows into my chest.

I guess we both have old wounds to keep us up here with the goats.

"What are you smiling about?" She asks when she picks her head up and catches the grin on my face.

"Sweetheart," I tell her, "I'm just so damn relieved you're not going to take that job and make me move away from the ridge."

"I have to take the job, Cypress." Her eyes are filled with sadness but I'm already kissing that away. "I can't afford to live without a job."

"Yes you can," I tell her, holding her face between my palms, "you're going to move in with me. I'm going to put a ring on your finger and we're going to give my folks more grand babies to babysit so we can sneak off and give them more grand babies. Your only job is taking my cock...and making sure Alfred doesn't wander into the street again. How's that sound?"

"Crazy." She laughs, "That sounds crazy. But I'll take it."

Violet spins around in my lap so she's straddling me and she digs her pussy down against my hard ridge as she kisses me. My hands are under her shirt, pulling her full breasts free from the cups of her bra and if the back door of the tavern didn't open just then, things were going to get interesting.

"Oh." A woman's voice that I don't recognize sounds mildly surprised to catch us in the state we're in. "Found 'em!" she calls back into the tavern, shutting the door and disappearing back inside before I have a chance to look up and see who she was.

"Who was that?" I whisper to Violet, reluctantly tucking her pretty tits back into her bra.

I might be resolved to spending more time with the clan, but we've seen enough of them tonight, I need to get my girl back in bed-- *our* bed.

"Pepper." Violet says it like it's common knowledge. "She works for Alice."

"My nan hired help?" I'm incredulous. Nan wouldn't even let us boys work for her on our summer vacations back in school. No one touches the general store but Nan.

Goodbyes are thrown out on our way to my truck with promises to arrive early for photos tomorrow before the ceremony.

"First, I am going to bend you over the kitchen table and make you scream so loud that Alfred comes to check on you," I promise Violet as we head back up the mountain. "Then you're going to fill me in on what else I don't know about what's going on with my own kin."

Violet giggles, running her hand up my thigh and over my already throbbing cock as I drive.

"Let's close the drapes and leave Alfred guessing."

Epilogue 1

The Next Day
Cypress

Standing up on a stage in front of half the town wearing a suit isn't my idea of a good time. The collar on this shirt is too tight, these boots aren't the good pair that's already broken in, and I know I'm fidgeting like a kid while my brother, Birch, repeats the vows as the preacher reads them.

My eyes are on Violet the whole time.

Her dress is a strapless gown in a burgundy color that shows off the natural bronze of her skin and a whole lot more of her ample cleavage that I'm happy about seeing on display in front of so many of Moonshine Ridge's unmarried males.

I'm happy I made it down for the wedding and I plan to celebrate my brother and his new bride's happiness with too much of the good food coming coming off of the Diaz grill and a red plastic cup or two from one of the kegs that Cedar donated to the cause, but before that, I need to get my girl alone.

Finally, the preacher pronounces them man and wife, Birch plants a liplock on Maggie that has her blushing a darker red than her bridesmaid's dresses, and we exit the stage two by two, running the gauntlet of flying birdseed in reverse order from how we got up here.

"Are your maid of honor duties over with now?" I get Violet in my arms as soon as we're free, pulling her to my chest so those beautiful breasts of hers are smashed up against me and all that pretty cleavage is for my eyes only.

"I have to make a toast later." She laughs when she sees me staring down Mesa and his brother Vale, making sure they know she's with me.

Let the Diaz boys get their own women.

"Where's your wrap, sweetheart? Let's go get you covered up before I have to start throwing punches at my old school buddies out here."

"Everyone knows I belong to you and only you," she scolds playfully but she doesn't argue when I drape the wide scarf in the matching deep red around her shoulders.

"Come with me." I tug her by the hand and I can already tell she's got some downright dirty thoughts going through her mind as she lets me lead her out behind Nan's old barn. But we don't stop there, I keep walking, all the way down to the edge of the stream that runs through Nan's property.

"You know I'm not much for an audience," I say by way of explanation when I get to the section where the water has eroded away the shore into a tiny beach.

I was out here early in the day, setting this up for us while she was busy getting ready with the other girls.

Right now, standing just behind Violet with my hands resting on her shoulders, I look at my handiwork and hope it looks romantic.

The solar lights flicker in the lanterns that I picked up from Ash in his sporting goods section. I had to weigh them down with some rocks but they're all still in place, making a semi circle around the picnic blanket-- also weighted down with some rocks-- covered with rose petals that mostly haven't managed to get blown away.

"Cypress." Violet breathes my name softly and I know I did a good job of making the place look special for her. "This is very fancy."

She slips off her shoes and steps onto the blanket. Then she turns around and gives me a wicked little wink that has me so ready to take her right here and now that I almost change my plans.

"Hang on, baby," I tell her, before she can distract me even more, "that's not why I brought you out here."

She drops her head and looks around at the blankets

and the lanterns and the roses and then back up and me with one eyebrow lifted.

But when I hit my knee in front of her, she can tell it's not because I'm about to get my head under her skirt. Not right away, at least.

"Violet Turner--" I didn't think I'd be nervous, but right now sweat is beading on my skin and there's a tingle running up my spine. My hands are shaking so bad I almost drop the little box that's been in my coat pocket all day.

"Ah hell, Vi." I huff out a long breath and pop the box open unceremoniously. "I'm no good at this stuff."

She's already got her hand held out for me though and I slip the ring on over the proper finger, relieved that it fits well enough till we can get it sized properly for her.

"Marry me, Vi."

"Of course I will," she answers, stroking her fingers through my hair and then lowering herself to her knees with me.

"I finally found my mountain man and I'm not letting you go now," she promises me as her fingers reach for my belt. "We should take advantage of some alone time before we're expected back at the party, don't you think?"

I think my girl has a point.

Epilogue 2

Ten Years Later
Violet

The fire crackles in the fireplace and snow falls outside the windows.

"Best I could do," my husband tells me, looking up from the pile of blankets and pillows he's arranged on the floor in front of the hearth.

It's our ten year anniversary and the snow has already been falling for a few days in early October.

"Come down here, wife," Cypress commands in his bossy voice, the one he knows I like to hear when he's about to fuck me senseless. "Let me get a taste of you. I want to have your cream coating my beard before I make you come on my cock."

It's not often we have the house all to ourselves

anymore and making love to my husband in front of the fire is something I miss.

We cut in line in front of Cedar and Cami, rushing to the courthouse on an impatient impulse one day about two weeks after Birch and Maggie tied the knot for an early October anniversary but it took us almost five years to get pregnant.

Not for lack of trying.

We went through some tests but the doctor down in Slow River said nothing was wrong, it was just taking time.

Watching my sisters-in-law having babies and getting to share that experience with each other was hard. I worried that by the time it was my turn, they'd be done having kids.

Fortunately it didn't work out that way. When I found out I was pregnant with Peony, both Cami and Maggie were pregnant with me. Then I had to spend most of my pregnancy with the boys in bed.

Alder and Aspen came out healthy and have been wreaking havoc since day one but Doctor Hart was adamant that my body's not likely to take another pregnancy so three is our limit.

Cypress says his baby brother, Ash and his wife, Hyacinth, can have the record at five. This is the second time Hy's gotten pregnant since having her tubes tied after number three. She says this time it's Ash's turn to get fixed.

Finding the Mountain Man

Dropping my robe on the floor, I sink down into the pallet of soft bedding that my husband has laid out.

Even after two pregnancies-- one with twins-- Cypress looks at me like I'm a centerfold model.

"Damn wife," he murmurs against my skin as he sinks his face between my breasts, "you are fucking sexy, baby."

And I know he means it.

Cypress lays me down, wraps my legs around his neck, and slides his tongue through my center till I'm panting and begging him to fuck me.

After ten years together, he's learned how to get me off fast-- and how to drag it out and make it last.

Tonight starts off fast, with me screaming his name so loud it bounces off the ceiling beams when he sucks my clit and has me riding his beard while I come hard the first time. Then I'm knocking him back and crawling over him, barely recovered from my first orgasm and already dripping wet and yearning to take his thick cock inside me.

We've got three days, plenty of firewood, and more snow in the forecast.

There's nowhere I'd rather spend our anniversary than right here in our family cabin with my mountain man.

Next from the Moonshine Ridge Mountain Men

The Jones Family

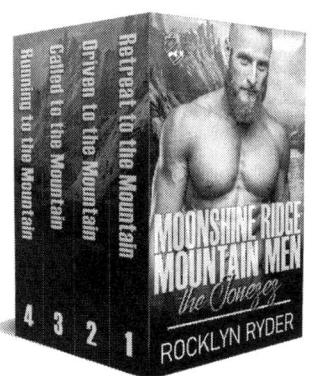

Meet the Jones Family beginning with
<u>*Retreat to the Mountain*</u>

Eddie Jones

Now that the rafting season is over, I won't need to leave Moonshine Ridge to go down to the big warehouse stores till next summer and that means doing more of my shopping locally.

Stepping inside the market, the bell on the door jingles, and I'm about to give Alice my customary greeting before grabbing a basket, when my head snaps back to the woman behind the counter.

The curvy brunette at the register is *not* the octogenarian store keeper that I've known my whole life and I know for a fact she doesn't belong to any of Alice's grandsons, the McAllister brothers, either.

Because this woman is *mine*.

Pepper's too young to have already suffered such big disappointment. She thinks her life is already over, but I'm here to show her that it's just beginning.

About the Author

Rocklyn prefers her romance reads to be short, cute, and dirty; low drama and a little over-the-top: extra points for growly, alpha heroes with beards.

Originally from the farms and ranches of Central California, Rocklyn grew up in the lap of the Sierra Nevada mountains. Those small towns will always be home, but Rocklyn was born to roam.

These days she spends her days exploring America's back roads in her camper trailer, writing steamy happily-ever-afters while looking for internet.

Keep in touch when you join her (mostly) weekly newsletter and never miss updates on what she has in the works-- and what's working and not in a life full of adventure and shenanigans.

Sign up at https://www.rocklynwrites.net

Printed in Dunstable, United Kingdom